HOW TO MELT
A FROZEN HEART

HOW TO MELT
A FROZEN HEART

BY

CARA COLTER

First published in Great Britain 2013
by Mills & Boon, an imprint of Harlequin (UK) Limited.
Large Print edition 2013
Harlequin (UK) Limited, Eton House,
18-24 Paradise Road, Richmond, Surrey TW9 1SR

ISBN: 978 0 263 23690 3

Harlequin (UK) policy is to use papers that are natural, renewable and recyclable products and made from wood grown in sustainable forests. The logging and manufacturing process conform to the legal environmental regulations of the country of origin.

Printed and bound in Great Britain
by CPI Antony Rowe, Chippenham, Wiltshire

To my favorite animal lover,
Margo Jakobsen,

and her beloved,
the true Prince of Pomerania, Phaut.

CHAPTER ONE

BRENDAN GRANT AWOKE with a start. At first he heard only the steady beat of rain on the roof, but then the phone rang again, shrill, jangling across his nerves. His eyes flicked to his bedside clock.

Three o'clock.

He felt his heart begin to beat a hard tattoo inside his chest. What good could ever come of a 3:00 a.m. phone call?

But then he remembered, and even though he remembered, he reached over and touched the place in the bed beside him. Two and a half years later and he still felt that ripple of shock at the emptiness. Becky was gone. The worst had already happened.

He groped through the darkness for the phone, picked it up.

"Yeah?" His voice was raspy with sleep.

"Charlie's dying."

And then the phone went silent in his hands.

Brendan lay there for a moment longer, holding the dead phone, not wanting to get up. He didn't really even like Charlie. They were going to start breaking ground on the lakeside living complex, Village on the Lake, tomorrow. His design had already attracted the attention of several architectural magazines, and based on the plan, the project had been nominated for the prestigious Michael Edgar Jonathon Award.

Still, as always, before they broke ground, and even after, he struggled with a feeling of it not being what he had wanted, missing the mark in some vague way he could not quite define. He recognized the stress was beginning. He was a man who needed his sleep.

But with a resigned groan, he sat up, swung his legs over the side of the bed, and sat there for a moment, his head in his hands, listening to the rain on the roof. He was so sick of rain.

He certainly didn't want to go out in it at three in the morning.

Then, with a sigh, Brendan reached for his jeans.

Ten minutes later, he was on Deedee's front stoop, hammering on her door. Her house was a two-minute drive from his. Brendan turned and looked out over his neighborhood. They both enjoyed locations on "The Hill," still Hansen's most prestigious neighborhood, and even on such a ghastly night the views were spectacular.

Through wisps of mist, he could see the whole city, pastel-painted turn-of-the-century houses nestled under mature maples, clinging to the sides of steep hills. Beyond the houses and the cluster of downtown buildings, lights penetrated the gloomy gray and reflected in the black, restless waters of Kootenay Lake.

Brendan turned back as the door opened a crack. Deedee regarded him suspiciously, as if there was a possibility that by some mean coincidence at the very same time she had called him, a home invader—Hansen's first—was waiting on her front stair to prey on the elderly.

Satisfied it was Brendan Grant in the flesh, she opened the door.

"Don't you look just like the devil?" she said. "Coming out of the storm like that, all dark menace and bristling bad temper. I used to say to Becky you had to have Black Irish in you somewhere. Or pure pirate."

Brendan stepped in and regarded his grand-mother-in-law with exasperated affection. Only Deedee would see a devil or a pirate in the doer of a good deed!

"I'll try to contain the bristling bad temper," he said drily. The darkness he could do noth-ing about. It was his coloring: dark brown eyes, dark brown hair, whiskers blacker than night. It was also his heart.

Deedee was ninety-two, under five feet tall, frighteningly thin. Still, despite the fact it was 3:15 in the morning and her cat, Charlie, was dying, she was dressed in her go-to-church best. She had on a pantsuit the color of pink grapefruit. A matching ribbon was tied in a bow in her snow-white curls.

Would Becky have looked like this someday? If she had grown old? The pain was sharp, his guilt so intense it felt as if a knife had been inserted underneath his ribs. But Brendan was accustomed to it coming like this, in unexpected moments, and he held his breath, waiting, watching himself, almost bemused.

Pain, but no emotion. A man so emotionally impoverished he had not shed a single tear for his wife.

Sometimes he felt as if his heart was a tomb that a stone had been rolled in front of, sealing it away forever.

"I'll get my coat," Deedee said. "I've already got Charlie in the cat carrier."

She turned to retrieve her coat—pink to match her outfit—from the arm of a sofa, and he saw Charlie glaring balefully at him from a homemade carrier that looked like a large and very ugly purse.

Charlie's head poked out a round hole, his ginger fur stuck up in every direction, his whiskers kinked, his eyes slit with dislike and bad temper. He made a feeble attempt to squeeze his gargantuan self out the tiny opening, but his quick resignation to defeat, and the raspy breathing caused by the effort, made Brendan aware that tonight was the end of the road for the ancient, cranky cat.

Deedee turned back to him, carefully buttoning her coat around her. Brendan picked up the cat carrier with one hand and crooked his other elbow. Deedee threaded her arm through his, and he nudged open the door with his knee, trying not to be impatient when the rain sluiced down his neck as she handed him a huge ring of keys.

"Lock the handle *and* the dead bolt," she ordered, as if they were in a high-crime area of New York City.

Both locks were sticky, and Brendan made a note to come by and give them a squirt of lubricant the next time he had a chance.

Finally they turned toward his car, inched

down the steep stairs that took them from her front stoop to the road. When they reached the flat walkway, he tried to adjust his stride to Deedee's tiny steps. He was just under six feet tall, his build lithe with a runner's sleekness rather than a bodybuilder's muscle, but Deedee made him feel like a giant.

A bristling pirate of a giant.

Brendan found himself wishing she would have called one of her children to accompany her on this late-night trip to the vet's office. But for a reason he couldn't quite decipher—it certainly wasn't his graciousness—it was him she turned to when she needed anything, from a lightbulb changed to her supply of liquid meal replacements restocked.

Deedee was not a nice little old lady. She was querulous, demanding, bossy, ungrateful and totally self-centered. It had occurred to Brendan more than once that she called him because no one else would come. But Deedee was his inheritance from his late wife. Becky and Deedee had adored each other. For that reason alone he came when she called.

Finally, he had both the cat and Deedee settled, the animal on the backseat, the woman in the front. The carrier did not look waterproof and he hoped the cat would not have an accident that would bleed through to the seat. Of course, with Charlie it might not be an accident. It might be pure spite.

Regardless, the car was brand-new, all plush leather and purring power. Had Brendan bought it hoping to fill some emptiness? If so, he had failed colossally, like putting a pebble in a hole left by a cannonball. Brendan shook off the thought, annoyed. It was the lateness of the night, the strangeness of being awake at what seemed to him to be the witching hour, that made him vulnerable to uncharacteristic introspection.

He got in the driver's side and started the engine, glanced at Deedee and frowned. She looked quite thrilled to be having this middle of the night outing, not like an old woman making the painful final journey with her cat.

"Which vet are you using? Is he expecting us?"

"I'll give you directions," she snapped.

It was the tone of voice she used right before she pronounced you an idiot, so he shrugged and put the car in drive, and pulled out into the wet, abandoned streets of Hansen.

He was determined to be patient. It was one more loss for her. Putting down her precious cat. She was entitled to be crabby tonight, and he did not want her to be alone at the vet's office as the needle went in. He did not want her to be alone when she came home without her cat.

She gave him directions, and he drove in silence, the mountains on either side of the valley making the night darker, the water hissing up under the tires. The cat's breathing was labored.

Deedee issued shrill commands for Brendan to slow down and squinted at the signs on every crossroad. Finally, she fished in her purse, took out a piece of paper and held it very close to her face.

"If you give me the address, this new car has GPS."

She contemplated that, deeply suspicious of technology, then reluctantly gave him the information.

He put it in his system. They were headed into the neighborhood that bordered Creighton Creek. A stone's throw from Hansen proper, the area was rural residential, with a collection of small, neat acreages. Because of the great location, and the land, it was a sought-after area for young professionals who had a dream of children, a golden retriever and a horse or two.

All Brendan had ever wanted, growing up the only child of a single mother, was that most elusive of things—normal. And when he'd been almost there, in a blink, everything was gone. There must have been something he could have done. Anything.

He felt the pain again, of being powerless, and again felt himself watching, wondering if at some unexpected moment he would just break open. If he did, he was certain it would shatter him, that the pieces would be so small there would be no collecting them and putting it all together again.

But no, he was able to focus on the small, old houses of Creighton Creek, which were slowly but surely being replaced with bigger ones. Brendan's firm, Grant Architects, had designed many of the newer homes, and he allowed himself, as they drove by one of his houses—one with a particularly complicated roofline—to be diverted from the painful realization of the life he was not going to have by the reality of the one he did.

The house was beautiful. The home owners loved it. Again, he had to try and shake that feeling of having *missed* something.

"I don't recall a vet located out here," he said. "In fact, didn't I take you and Charlie to Doc Bentley recently?"

"Dr. Bentley is an idiot," Deedee muttered. "He told me to put Charlie to sleep. That there was no hope at all. 'He's old. He's got cancer. Let him go.'" She snorted. "I'm old. Are you just going to let me go? Put me to sleep, maybe?"

Brendan cast Deedee a glance. Carefully, he said, "Isn't that what we're doing? Taking Charlie to have him put to, er, sleep?"

Deedee cranked her head toward him and gave him a withering look. "I am taking him to a healer."

Brendan didn't like the sound of that, but he carefully tried to strip any judgment from his voice. "What do you mean, a healer?"

"Her name's Nora. She has that new pet rescue place. Babs Taylor told me she has a gift."

"A gift," he repeated.

"Like those old-time preachers who laid their hands on people."

"Are you kidding me?" He began to look for a place to turn around. "You need a vet. Not a nut."

"What I need is a miracle, and Dr. Bentley already told me he can't give me one." Deedee's voice was high and squeaky. "Babs's niece volunteers out there. She said somebody brought in a dog that was deader than a doornail. And Nora Anderson brought it back to life. With her *energy*."

Brendan felt his mouth tighten in a hard line of cynicism. One thing Becky and her grandmother had had in common? They loved all things "woo-woo." They actually believed in what they called psychics and mediums, had frowned at him when he had made disparaging remarks about fortune-tellers and gypsies.

An unfortunate mental picture of Nora was forming in his mind: dangling earrings, wildly colored head scarf, hideous makeup, dark blue eye shadow, a slash of blood-red on her lips.

"Can you keep a secret?" Deedee didn't wait for him to respond, but lowered her voice conspiratorially, as if dozens could hear. "Clara, over at the post office, told me she thinks from the mail that she gets that Nora is Rover. You know, from the column? *Ask Rover?*"

He didn't know.

"You can tell when you read it," Deedee elaborated, still whispering. "Nora gets right inside their heads. The animals."

"That must be helpful, so that she knows where to send the energy to," he said, his tone deeply sarcastic. Deedee missed the sarcasm entirely, because she went on with enthusiasm.

"Exactly! I'm a great fan of *Ask Rover,* so I knew she was the one who could help Charlie. I don't drive anymore," Deedee said, as if Brendan, her favored chauffeur, didn't know that, "and I can't hear properly on the phone, so I wrote her a letter, and brought it right to the post office so I knew she'd get it the next day. She wrote me back right away saying she would send me—Charlie—some energy."

Brendan felt a kind of helpless fury claw at him. Deedee nursed the worry that Hansen's first home invader would target her. She double-locked her doors. She was suspicious of the checkout girl at the grocery counting out the wrong change! How could she fall for this?

"It worked," Deedee whispered. "Charlie got better. But then he got worse again, and she wouldn't answer my letters. I phoned, too, even though I can't hear, but I got an answering machine. I hate those. No one returned my calls. Then tonight, Charlie's breathing changed. I'm scared. I know he's dying."

Brendan hated it that she was scared, and hated it more that her fear had made her so vulnerable. "Did you send money?"

The silence was telling.

"Did you?"

"A little."

His GPS system startled them both by telling him to turn right at the next crossroad. Suddenly he wanted very much to meet the person who would use an elderly woman's fear over losing her beloved pet to bamboozle money out of her.

All the better if they rousted her from a deep sleep in the middle of the night!

He turned right; they went up a road he had never noticed before, and passed under an archway that spanned the road.

A sign hung from the archway, letters painted in fresh, primary colors. Nora's Ark.

At any other time, he might have thought it was clever little play on words. Or maybe not. He didn't like *cute.* He was an architect. He liked calculation, precision, math. He liked figuring out how large a load a beam could carry, and how to make a wall of glass that was structurally sound.

He liked the completely balanced marriage of art and science that was his work. If at the end of the project he always felt, somehow, he had missed the mark, wasn't that part of what drove him to do even better the next time? To try again for that thing, whatever it was, that was just out of his reach?

Brendan considered himself pragmatic and practical, perhaps with a good measure of cynical thrown in. He was the man least likely to give himself over to whimsy. But given that it seemed to have been raining for forty days and forty nights, he felt a strange shiver along his spine that he was arriving at an ark of any sort.

Below the sign Nora's Ark was a smaller one, announcing they were supported by the Hansen Community Betterment Committee.

His company was one of the charter members!

He shook off his annoyance, and drove over a wooden bridge that spanned a creek that was still raging with spring runoff, though it was the last day of June. Up ahead, carved out of the mountainous wilderness all around, a white house—almost a cottage—was illuminated in his headlights, surrounded by a picket fence and a yard where yellow climbing roses rioted.

Through the grim, pelting rain a light shone, warm and inviting, from inside, and the house seemed like a welcoming place, not the kind of place where a charlatan who cheated vulnerable old women would live.

Was someone awake? It was probably a good time for chanting and consulting cards. Though why do it if the mark wasn't there?

Behind the house and yard, barely visible in darkness that was slowly giving way to a soggy predawn, he could see the huge silhouette of a barn.

"Oh, we're here," Deedee breathed happily. "It looks just the way I thought it would."

That explained the appearance of the place. Homey. Welcoming. Like the old witch's cottage in *Hansel and Gretel.*

All the better to dupe people, to lure them closer.

"You wait here," Brendan said, and cut off Deedee's protest with a firm slam of the car door. He walked up a path that smelled of perfume as he crushed damp fallen rose petals under his feet.

Then, out of the corner of his eye, back toward the barn, he saw a light fly up, heard the high-pitched whinny of a horse, and, straining against the sounds of the storm, he was sure he heard the startled cry of someone in trouble. A female in trouble.

CHAPTER TWO

TURNING FROM THE house, adrenaline pumping, his instincts on red alert, Brendan Grant ran toward the barn.

At first, he thought it was a pile of old rags in the churned-up mud of the paddock adjoining the barn. The pile was faintly illuminated by the fallen flashlight beside it. Then it moved. Heedless of the mud, he put one hand on the fence, leaped it, landed, raced to the still form. It looked like a child facedown in the mud.

His sense of urgency surged as he squatted down. He knew better than to try to move whoever it was without assessing the injuries.

"Are you all right?"

Movement from the heap of rags and a squeak of distressed surprise were a relief to Brendan. Then the pile of rags flipped over.

It was his turn to be shocked. It wasn't a child, but a woman. Her hair reminded him of Charlie's—ginger, sticking up all over the place, except where a clump of mud had flattened it to her skull. But even the mud that streaked her skin could not hide the exquisite loveliness of her pale face.

Her nose was dainty, faintly dusted with copper freckles. Her lips were plump and pink; her chin had a little jut to it that hinted at a stubborn temperament. A goose egg was rising alarmingly above her right eye.

Her eyes were amazing, wide-spaced, unusually large in the smallness of her face, a color of jade that flickered with light in the grayness of the night.

If this was Nora she was an enchantress of the kind who would have no need of makeup to weave her spell.

She was obviously very woozy, because she looked at him quizzically, and then oddly, reached up and touched his cheek, a faint smile on her face, as if she did not see a dark devil arrived on the tails of the storm, but something else entirely. Something that she recognized and welcomed.

His feeling of being enchanted—however reluctantly—increased.

Then abruptly she came to her senses. She seemed to realize she was flat on her back in the middle of the night, in the mud, with a strange man who oozed menace and bristling bad temper hovering over her.

Her eyebrows knit together in consternation and she struggled to sit up.

"Hey," he said, his attempt at a soothing tone coming out of his mouth like rust, a hoarse croak. "Try not to move."

She looked as if she had no intention of following his well-meaning instruction, so he laid a hand on her shoulder. It was tiny underneath a thin jacket that appeared to be soaking up rain rather than repelling it.

He could see a little bow on what could be her pajamas at the V of her jacket.

She shook off his hand, sat up, wincing from

the effort. He'd been right about her chin giving a clue to her temperament. She was stubborn.

"Who are you?" she demanded. "What are you doing out here, on my property, at this time of night?"

He was annoyed with himself that the tone of her voice increased the sense of enchantment weaving through this miserable night. Despite the lack of welcome in her words, her voice reminded him of maple syrup, rich and smooth and sweet.

She scanned his face, that initial reaction of trust, of welcome, completely gone. Now she looked wary and stubborn and maybe just a little frightened.

What she didn't have was the look of a person who would be trying to dupe an old lady out of her money.

No sense putting off the moment of truth.

"Are you Nora?"

She nodded. He let that sink in. No head scarf. No dangling earrings. Certainly no blue eye shadow, or slash of red at her mouth.

Brendan was aware that in a very short time he had started to hope the woman in a vulnerable little heap in the mud was not the same woman who had written Deedee a letter promising to heal her cat. With energy. For a fee.

He looked at her fresh face, tried to imagine dangling earrings and heavy makeup and the gypsy scarf, and found his imagination didn't quite go that far. But fresh faced or not, she'd duped Deedee. He was already disillusioned by life, so why be disturbed by the gathering of a little more evidence?

Still, for the moment she looked faintly frightened, and he felt a need to alleviate that.

"I brought a cat out," he said. "I heard a ruckus out here, saw a light and came to investigate."

She considered his explanation, but looked doubtful. He suspected he didn't look much like the kind of guy who would be attached to his cat.

"I heard you were a healer." He tried to strip judgment from his tone, but he must have looked even less like the kind of guy who would put any kind of faith in a healer than one who would be attached to a cat, because her doubtful expression intensified.

"Who did you hear that from?" she asked uneasily. Her eyes skittered toward the fence, as if she was going to try and make an escape.

"Deedee Ashton."

The name did not seem to register, but then she might be struggling to remember her own name at the moment.

"Can you tell me what happened?" he asked.

She put a hand to the goose egg above her eye.

"I don't know for sure," she said. "The horses might have knocked me over."

He scanned the corral. Three horses were squeezed against the back fence, restless and white-eyed. He didn't know much about horses, but these ones seemed in no way docile.

He told himself firmly that it was none of his business what kind of chances she took. He didn't know her. He certainly didn't care about her. Still, there was a certain kind of woman that could make a man feel he should be protective. That was the kind you really had to guard against, especially if you had already failed in the department of protecting the smaller and weaker and more vulnerable.

Brendan ordered himself not to comment. But, of course, his mouth disobeyed his mind.

"Given you're about the size of a peanut, doesn't it seem a touch foolhardy to decide to come mingle with your wild mustangs in the middle of the night?"

She glared at him. Her look clearly said *don't tell me what to do,* which was fair.

"Unless, of course, you hoped your *energy* was going to tame them?"

Those amazing eyes narrowed. "What do you know about my energy?"

"Not as much as I plan to."

"Why does that sound like a threat?" she asked.

He shrugged.

She tossed her head at that, but he saw a veil drop smoothly over the flash of fire in those green eyes, as if *he* had hurt *her* by being a doubter. You'd think, in her business, she would have developed a thicker skin.

But he would have to deal with all that later. She had begun to shiver from being wet, but when she tried to move, a small groan escaped her lips.

He knew he shouldn't move her. But she was clearly freezing. Now was not the time to confront her about any claims she had made to Deedee. He shrugged out of his coat and wrapped it around her.

She looked as if she planned to protest his act of chivalry, but when he tucked his coat around her, he could clearly see the warmth seduced her. She snuggled inside it instead. She looked innocent, about as threatening as a wounded sparrow.

Stripping away any censure he felt about her claims of extraordinary power, he said, "Can you move your hands? How about your feet? Can you turn your head from side to side for me?"

"What are you? A doctor?" Despite the protest, she tested each of her body parts as he named it.

He touched the ugly-looking bump rising above her right eye. She winced.

"You're not lucky enough to have conjured up a doctor. You'll have to work on your conjuring a little. I'm an architect. Luckily, I have a little construction site first aid experience."

As he had hoped, at the mention of his profession—oh, those professional men were so trustworthy—her wariness of him faded, though annoyance at his conjuring remark had turned her green eyes to slits that reminded him of Charlie.

He picked the flashlight out of the mud and shone it in her eyes, looking for pupil reaction.

"Tell me about your cat," she said, swatting at the light.

"So you can send him energy?"

"Why are you here, if you're so cynical?"

He felt a shiver along his spine, similar to what he had felt when he passed under the ark sign. What if he hadn't come along when he had? Would she have lain in the mud until she had hypothermia? Would the horses have trampled her?

But he was certainly not going to let her see that for a moment he was in the sway of an idea that some power he did not understand might have drawn him here at the exact moment she needed him.

Ridiculous. If such a power existed, where had it been the night Becky had needed it?

He actually saw Nora flinch, and realized he had grimaced. It no doubt gave him the pirate look that Deedee had seen earlier.

Keeping his tone level, Brendan said, "I'm here as the result of a comedy of errors. I thought I was on my way to a legitimate practitioner of animal medicine."

"With your cat."

He nodded.

"You don't really look like a cat kind of guy."

"No? What do cat kind of guys look like?"

She studied him, the eyes narrow again. "Not like you," she said decisively.

"So, what do I look like? A rottweiler kind of guy? Bulldog? Boxer?"

Her look was intense. If a person believed that energy crap, they would almost think she was reading his. He raised the light again, shining it in her eyes, hoping to blind her. He was not sure he liked the sensation of being *seen*.

"You're not a dog kind of guy, either."

Accurate, but not spookily so.

"In fact," she continued, "I'd be surprised if you even had a plant."

Okay. That was about enough of that.

"I never said it was *my* cat." He turned off the light and put it in his pocket. "I don't think your back is injured, so I'm going to pick you up and carry you to the house."

"You are not picking me up! I'll walk." She tried to find her feet, and glared at him as if the fact that it was his jacket swimming around her stopped her from doing so. "If you'll just give me your hand—"

But Brendan did not just give her a hand. It wasn't the jacket. The small effort of trying to get up had made her turn a ghostly white, the freckles and mud standing out in stark relief. So he ignored her protests, slid his arms under her shoulders and her knees and scooped her up easily.

She was tiny, like that wounded sparrow, and despite the barrier of his jacket, he was aware of an unusual warmth oozing out of her where he held her against his chest.

Was it because it had been so long since he had touched another human being that he felt an unwelcome shiver of pleasure?

CHAPTER THREE

UNEASILY HOLDING A beautiful stranger in his arms and feeling that unwanted shiver of something good, Brendan Grant was aware it was what he had wanted to feel when he had purchased the car. Just a moment's pleasure at something. Anything. With the car, he had not even come close.

He should have already learned *stuff* could never do it. An unwanted memory came, of standing in front of the house he now owned, with Becky at his side, thinking, *This is the beginning of my every dream come true.*

"Put me down!"

Nora's hand, smacking hard against his chest, brought him gratefully back to the here and now.

"You couldn't even stand up by yourself," he

said, unmoved by her tone. "I'll put you down in a minute. When I get you to the house."

Her expression was mutinous, but she winced, suddenly in pain, and conceded with ill grace.

He strode to the house. The woman in his arms was rigid with tension for a few seconds, then relaxed noticeably. He glanced down at her to make sure she hadn't passed out.

Wide green eyes stared up at him, defiant, unblinking. If ever there were eyes that could cast a spell, it would be those ones!

Just as he got close the porch light came on, illuminating the fact that Deedee had grown tired of waiting, had exited the passenger seat of the car and was feebly trying to wrestle her cat carrier out of the back.

A boy, at that awkward stage somewhere between twelve and fifteen, who also had ginger hair like Charlie's, exploded out the front door of the cottage, and the woman in Brendan's arms squirmed to life.

His architect's mind insisted on filling in

pieces of the puzzle as he looked at the boy: too old to be hers.

"Put me down," she insisted, then shook herself as if waking from a dream. "Honestly! I told you I could walk."

The boy looked as if he had been sleeping, his hair flat against his face on one side and sticking straight up on the other. But he was now wide-awake and ready to fight.

"You heard her," he said, "put her down. Who are you? What have you done to my aunt Nora?"

Not his mother. His aunt.

The boy dashed back into the house and came out wielding a coat rack. He held it over his shoulder, like a baseball bat he was prepared to swing. His level of menace was laughable. Brendan was careful not to show that he had rarely felt less threatened.

Still, he couldn't help but admire a kid prepared to do battle with a full-grown man.

Brendan closed his eyes, and was suddenly aware he didn't feel the weight of new cynicism. Instead he was acutely aware of how the sweet weight in his arms and the woman's warmth were making his skin tingle. He was aware that the air smelled of rain and rose petals, and that those smells mingled with the clean scent of her hair and her skin.

Two and a half years ago, in the night, a phone call had changed everything forever. He'd been sleepwalking through life ever since, aware that he was missing something essential that other people had. That it was locked inside the tomb, and that even if he could have rolled the rock away, he was not sure that he would.

And now, another middle of the night phone call, leading to this moment. He was standing here in a stranger's yard with a woman who either was trouble, or was in trouble, in his arms, an adolescent boy threatening him with a coat rack, Deedee oblivious to it all, struggling to get her dying cat out of the car.

Brendan was aware that the rock had rolled, that a crack of light had appeared in the darkness. He was aware of feeling wide-awake, as if he was a warrior waiting to see if it was a friend or foe outside.

For the first time in more than two years he felt the blood racing through his veins, the exquisite touch of raindrops on his skin. For the first time in so long, Brendan knew he was alive.

And it didn't make him happy.

Not one little bit.

Instead, he felt deeply resentful that the prison of numbness that had become his world was being penetrated by this vibrant, demanding capricious energy called life.

"Put me down!" Nora insisted again, hoping for a no-nonsense tone of voice that would hide the confusion she was really feeling.

She looked up into the exquisite strength of the stranger's face. Through the fabric of the expensive rain jacket he had wrapped around her, she could feel the iron hardness of his chest where she leaned into it. His arms, cradling her shoulders and her legs, were bands of pure steel.

She should have fought harder against being picked up and toted across the yard like a sleeping baby. Because it was crazy to feel so safe.

The stranger had a certain cool and dangerous aloofness about him. He had already made it clear he had heard some exaggerated claim about her energy that had allowed him to put her in the category of gypsies, tramps and thieves.

So the feeling of safety had to be attributed to the terrible knock on her head. Being in his arms made Nora achingly aware that she had been alone for a while now. Carrying the weight of her world all by herself. It was a relief to be carried for a change. A guilty pleasure, but a relief nonetheless.

Now, looking up at him, she could feel something shifting. His hands tightened marginally on her and some finely held tension played around the corners of his sinfully sensuous mouth.

The soft suede of his deep, deliciously brown eyes had not changed when he had called her a healer, his tone accusatory, but now they had hardened to icy remoteness and sparked with vague anger.

Well, he had come to her rescue and was being threatened with a coat rack. Naturally, he would react.

But now he was not the man she had awoken to, one with something so compelling in his face she had reached up and touched…

She shook that off, striving for the control she had lost when she'd accepted his arms around her, accepted being cradled against the fortress of his chest, accepted the comfort of being carried.

She could not be weak. She had to be strong. Everything was relying on *her* now. She was completely on her own since her fiancé had said, "Look, it's him or it's me."

Surely, when her sister had appointed her guardian of then fourteen-year-old Luke she had not expected that turn of events! Karen had thought she was entrusting her son to a home, to a stable, financially secure environment that would have two parents, one her sister, Nora, affectionately known within the family as "the flake," the other a highly respected stable person, a vet with his own practice.

But the highly predictable world Karen had envisioned for Luke didn't happen. When everything had fallen apart between her and Vance, Nora had risked it all on a new start.

She *had* to be strong.

"Look," Nora said, "you really have to put me down."

The man ignored her, looking flintily past her to Luke.

To get his attention off her nephew, and to show she meant business, she smacked the stranger hard, against the solid wall of his chest. It felt ineffectual, as if she was being annoying, like a bug, not powerful like a lioness.

Still, when his arm slid out from under her knees, and she found herself standing, albeit a bit wobbly, on her own two feet, instead of feeling relieved she felt the oddest sense of loss.

He had carried her across her yard with incredible ease, his stride long, powerful and purposeful, his breath remaining steady and even. It was the kind of strength a person might want to rely on.

If that person hadn't made a pact to rely totally on herself!

Get a grip, Nora ordered silently, moving away from the man. She was genuinely relieved that Luke dropped the coat rack and came to her side.

Casting a look loaded with suspicion and warning at the man who had carried her, Luke got his shoulder under her arm and helped her toward the house.

"What happened? Did he hurt you?"

"No. No. It wasn't him. I couldn't sleep and I went to check the animals. One of the new horses must have spooked and knocked me over."

"Why would you go out in the corral by yourself?" Luke asked.

"My question precisely." The man's voice was deep and calm, steady.

"Those horses were wild when they were

brought in," Luke said accusingly. "That one took a kick at the guy unloading him."

She didn't like it one little bit that it felt as if the two were forming an alliance against her!

Why had she gone into the corral when the horses were so restless? Probably she hadn't even thought about it, overly confident in her ability to calm animals.

Since she was a little girl she had found refuge from her mother and father's constant bickering by bringing home broken things to fix. Tiny wounded birds, abandoned cats, dogs near death.

Inside, Nora was still the girl who had been seen by family and school chums as an eccentric, a kook, and she was more comfortable hiding her gifts than revealing them.

Which made her very uncomfortable with whatever this stranger thought he knew about her.

Would Karen have ever made her guardian of Luke if she knew Vance would not be in the picture? Probably not. She would have known her sister could not be trusted to control impulses like jumping into a corral full of flighty horses in the middle of the night!

Nora was solely responsible for Luke. What if he'd found her out there in the mud? Hadn't he been traumatized enough? She was supposed to be protecting him!

Still, it was unsettling to her that what she remembered, in far more detail than her lapse of judgment before entering the corral, or the moments before being knocked over and knocked out, was the moment after.

Coming to, Nora had opened her eyes to find this man bent over her. His expression was intense, and he was breathtakingly handsome. Dark, thick hair was curling wetly around perfect features—a straight nose; whisker-roughened cheeks; a faintly cleft chin; firm, sensuous lips.

A raindrop had slid with exquisite slowness down his temple, over the high ridge of his cheekbone, onto his lip.

And then, in slow motion, it had fallen from his lip to hers.

Perhaps it was the knock on the head that had made the moment feel suspended, made the raindrop feel as if it sizzled in the chill of the night. Made her reach out with the tip of her tongue and taste that tiny pearl of water.

Perhaps it was the knock on the head that made her feel like a princess coming awake to find the prince leaning over her.

Through it all, Nora had been caught hard by eyes that mesmerized: velvet brown suede flecked with gold, a light in them that was mostly solid strength, with just the faintest shadow of something else.

Something she of all people should know.

Woozily, she had reached out and let the palm of her hand caress his bristly cheek, to touch that common ground she recognized between them.

He had gone very still under her touch, but he did not move away from it. She had felt a lovely sense of safety, that this was someone she could rely on.

But then the wooziness was gone, just like that, and she'd remembered she was in her paddock. And that she was alone out there with a man who had no business being on her property at this time of the night.

Nora's instincts when it came to animals were beyond good. Some people, including her ex-fiancé, Dr. Vance Height, whom she had met while working as an assistant in his veterinary practice, were spooked by what she could accomplish with sheer intuition.

But Vance was a reminder that Nora's good instincts did not extend to men. Or much else about life. With tonight being an unsettling exception, her perception was fabulous when it came to dealing with hurt, frightened animals.

Or writing her quirky, off-beat column *Ask Rover,* a column she had never admitted she was behind, because she had come across Vance reading it in her early days at his office, and he had been terribly scornful of it.

The intuition was not so good at helping her stretch her modest income from the column to support both the animal shelter and Luke. Thankfully, as the shelter became more established it was starting to receive financial support from the community of Hansen.

Her intuition was also not proving the least helpful at dealing with a now fifteen-year-old nephew who seemed intent on visiting his hurt and anger over the death of his mother on the whole world.

Feeling foolish now for that vulnerable moment when she had reached up and let her hand scrape the seductive whiskery roughness of the stranger's cheek, and more foolish for allowing herself to be carried across her yard by a perfect stranger, Nora shook off Luke's arm. She was supposed to be protecting him, not the other way around.

She turned and faced the man, folding her arms over her chest.

She had been, she was certain, mistaken that they shared anything in common. Looking at him from this angle, she found he looked hard and cold, and she had, as was her unfortunate habit, given her trust too soon.

"Where did he come from?" Luke asked in a suspicious undertone.

For all she knew he could be an ax murderer! Anyone could say they were an architect! She ran an animal rescue center. Anyone could say they had brought a cat.

She knew he wasn't a cat person, one likely to be ruled by the kind of sentiment that would drive him out on a night like this for the well-being of a cat.

But behind the man, she suddenly became aware of an old woman in a ghastly pink outfit. As Nora watched, the woman gave a grunt of exertion and freed a large container from the backseat of a car that was as gray as the night and sleek with sporty expense. The man turned to her, stepped back and took a large carpet bag from her.

Nora registered two things at once: how protective he seemed of that tiny, frail woman, and that there was indeed a cat! Its head was sticking out of a kind of window in the side of the carrier. One didn't have to have any psychic ability at all to know the cat did not have now, and probably never had had, a pleasing personality.

"I'm Brendan Grant," he said.

The name seemed Scottish to Nora, and with the rain plastering his hair to his head, running unchecked down the formidable, handsome lines of his face, it was just a little too easy to picture him as a Scottish warrior. Strong. Imperious to the weather.

Determined to get his own way.

What was his own way?

"And this is my grandmother, Deedee, and her cat, Charlie." The faint hiss of angry energy seemed to intensify around him. His mouth had become a hard line. He was watching Nora closely for her reaction.

"I'm sorry?" she said. What on earth was he doing here at this time of the night with his grandmother and her cat?

Still, whatever it was, it did dilute some of the threat she felt. Though not an expert, she was still fairly certain architect ax murderers did not travel with an entourage that included grandmothers and cats.

His voice calm and ice-edged, he said, "Deedee has been made certain promises concerning Charlie. And she has paid in advance."

Nora didn't have a clue what he meant. But she did realize the threat she felt was not of the ax-murderer variety.

It was of the raindrop-falling-from-lips variety. She was aware her head hurt, but was not at all sure this feeling of being caught off balance was caused by the knock to her head.

"I don't know what you're talking about," she said firmly.

She became aware that something rippled through Luke. She felt more than saw his discomfort. She cast her nephew a glance out of the corner of her eye.

Uh-oh.

"Look," the man said quietly, the commanding tone of his voice drawing her attention firmly back to him. "You may be able to pull the wool over the eyes of an old woman, but I'm here to look after her interests. And you should know that if you've swindled her, you can kiss the support of the Hansen Community Betterment Committee good-bye."

Kiss the support of the Hansen Community Betterment Committee good-bye? Nora couldn't let her panic show.

"Swindled your grandmother?" she asked instead. Below the panic, she could feel the insult of it! His caustic remarks about her energy and her being a healer were beginning to make an awful kind of sense.

"I wouldn't be surprised if the police became involved," Brendan said, the quiet in his voice making it all the more threatening.

CHAPTER FOUR

THE POLICE? NORA felt a sense of panic, as if her world were tilting.

Still, she could not cave before him. She was about to insist that he was the one trespassing on private property, except that at the mention of the police, she realized she wasn't the only one panicking.

Nora saw Luke go rigid.

There'd been an unfortunate incident at school involving the police way too recently.

Luke claimed to have *borrowed* a bicycle. Apparently without the full understanding of the bicycle's owner, which was why the police had become involved. Luke had talked to the other boy, and the whole thing, thankfully, had blown over.

Now her nephew met her eyes, pleading, and

then ducked his head, drawing a pattern in the wet ground with his bare toe.

Nora glanced back at Brendan Grant and saw he had not missed a thing. He was watching Luke narrowly, and her sense of him being a warrior intensified. His look did not bode well for her nephew.

What had Luke done now? She was acutely aware of having failed in her responsibility to her nephew by going into the corral by herself tonight. Now every protective instinct rose in her.

"Nobody swindled me," Deedee said plaintively. "She sent me energy for Charlie."

"For a price," Brendan added softly.

Nora knew she had not sent anyone any energy. And certainly not for a price! But Luke was squirming so uncomfortably she wanted to hit him with her elbow to make him stop drawing attention to himself.

Because no matter what he had done, Luke was no match for Brendan Grant. Not in any way. Not physically, nor could her poor orphaned nephew bear up under the anger that sparked in the man's eyes.

Taking a deep breath, she said brightly. "Oh, I remember now. Charlie."

Luke cast her a glance loaded with gratitude and relief, and she might have allowed herself to relish that, especially coupled with the fact he had taken up a coat rack in her defense. Moments when her nephew actually seemed to like her were rare, after all.

But Brendan Grant looked hard and skeptical, and she needed to stay focused on the immediate threat of that.

She put together the few clues she had. One of her gifts was an acute ability to focus on detail. Brendan and Deedee had arrived in the middle of the night. From what she could see of the cat, he was ill, the lateness of the hour suggested desperately so.

"Charlie's been sick, right?" she said.

"That's right!" Deedee said eagerly.

Brendan's expression just became more grim.

"You said you'd send him energy," Deedee

reminded her. "You said to send money. I sent fifty dollars."

"Fifty dollars?" Brendan snapped. "Deedee! You said you sent a *little* money."

"In terms of what my cat is worth to me, that is a small amount." The woman gave him a look that was equal parts sulk and steel.

"So there you have it," Brendan said to Nora, exasperated. "If you play your cards right, she'll sign over her house to you. You won't need the support of the Hansen Community Betterment Committee. Is that how this operation of yours works?"

"Of course not!" Nora said, feeling the heat rising in her cheeks. "I'm sure it was just a mistake. I must have thought the money was a donation."

She tried to keep her voice steady, but was not sure she succeeded.

"Uh-huh." He sounded cynical, and rightfully so.

Nora wanted to whirl on Luke and shake him. She had never even raised her voice to him, but their whole future was at stake here. And worse, if he had sent that letter, and taken that money—and who else could it possibly be?—he had stolen from a vulnerable old woman. How could he? Who was he becoming? And why couldn't she stop it?

Again she felt the weight of responsibility for her choices. Karen would have never entrusted her to raise her nephew alone. She would have been able to predict this catastrophe coming.

With great care, Nora kept herself from looking askance at her nephew.

"Let's get in out of the rain," she suggested, trying to keep her voice steady. Because he had given her his jacket, the rain had soaked through Brendan's shirt, which was now practically transparent.

She was aware she didn't really want Brendan Grant, with his bristling masculine energy and wet, clinging shirt, invading her house. She'd been here only a little while, but it had quickly become a sanctuary to her. On the other hand, she desperately needed to buy some time, to take Luke aside and figure out what he had done.

And fix it.

Yet again.

But a glance at the unyielding features of the man who had made her feel momentarily so safe told her this might not be so easy to fix.

The house was not what Brendan expected of a charlatan's house. There were no crystals dangling in the door wells and no clusters of herbs hanging upside down from their stems. There was no cloying scent of incense.

"Lovely," Deedee breathed with approval, standing in the doorway, taking it in.

"Disappointing," Brendan said.

In fact, he found the house was cozy and clean. An uneasiness crawled along his neck as they passed through a living room where a pair of love seats the color of melted butter faced each other across a coffee table where some of those yellow roses from the yard floated in a clear glass bowl.

"Disappointing?" Nora asked.

"No black cat. No cauldron on the hearth."

Nora shot him a look. She really was the cutest little thing. Again he had that feeling of coming awake. He didn't want to notice her, but how could he not? Her hair was a mess, standing straight up, strawberry-blonde dandelion fluff. Her eyes were huge in a dainty mud-streaked face. She looked more frightened now than when he had first found her.

The scam revealed. But her shock seemed genuine, and so did her distress.

"Look," Nora said in a defensive undertone, "I take in sick and abandoned animals. I don't claim to be a healer."

Her nephew snorted at that, and she shot him a glare that he was completely oblivious to.

Deedee, deaf anyway, hadn't even heard.

"As for black cats and cauldrons, I certainly don't do witchcraft!"

Her muddy, soaked clothes, and his jacket, swam around her, and he guessed she would be determined not to remove her coat and reveal the pajamas underneath.

He wasn't sure why. The pajama bottoms, which he could see, were filthy, but underneath the mud they were plaid. Utilitarian rather than sexy.

They came to the kitchen, and Nora turned on a light to reveal old cabinets painted that same cheerful shade of yellow as her sofas and roses. The floor was old hardwood planking that gleamed with patina. He smelled fresh bread.

There was a jar full of cookies on the counter, and notes and pictures were held by magnets to the front of a vintage fridge. There was a wood-burning stove in one corner, and an old, scarred oak table covered with schoolbooks.

The uneasiness returned. He thought of those wonders of granite and steel that people wanted for their kitchens these days, that he designed, and suddenly he knew what the uneasiness was. They somehow had all missed the mark.

For all the awards that decorated the walls of his office, he had never achieved *this*. A feeling.

He shook it off, looked back at Nora. The caption under her high school yearbook picture had probably read "Least likely to bamboozle an old woman out of her money."

But somebody had. The nephew? The kid practically had a neon sign over his head that flashed Guilty, but on the other hand, didn't all kids that age look like that? Slinky and defensive and as if they had just finished committing a crime?

What surprised Brendan was that he was interested at all in who did it. And if it was her nephew, to what lengths she would go to protect him.

But that's what happened when you came alive. Life, the interactions of people, their relationships and motivations interested you.

It was a wound waiting to happen, he warned himself.

"Put the cat there." Nora pointed to a kitchen island, a marble top fastened to solid wooden legs, and he set the cat carrier down, surreptitiously checking the bottom for any dampness that might have transferred to the seat of his new car.

He knew it said something about the kind of person he was that he was relieved to find none.

"He's been very sick," Deedee said. "Just like I told you in the letter."

"Maybe you could remind me what you wrote in your letter."

In the light of the kitchen, Brendan could see a knob growing alarmingly on Nora's forehead. She was wet and covered in mud.

And Brendan Grant was surprised there was a part of him that still knew the right thing to do. And was prepared to do it.

"The cat will have to wait," he heard himself say firmly, in the tone of voice he used on the construction site when a carpenter was insisting something couldn't be done the way he wanted it done.

And the people in the room reacted about the same way. Deedee swung her head and glared at him. Nora looked none too happy, either.

"I want to take a look at you," he insisted. "If

you don't need a trip to the emergency ward, you certainly need a shower and a change of clothes before you check out the cat."

"I can have a look at the cat first."

So she wanted what he wanted. For this to be quick. Look at the cat. Tell them what they all already knew about Charlie's prospects for a future. Of course, what they wanted parted ways at finding out who was guilty of taking money from Deedee, and what the consequences were going to be.

Still, handled properly, the whole drama could unfold and conclude in about two minutes, in and out.

Heavy on the out part. He wanted to head home and go back to bed.

His old life—that cave that was comforting in its lack of intensity, in its palette of grays—beckoned to him. But it seemed to him that nothing was going to go quite as he wanted.

Which he hated in and of itself. Because one thing Brendan Grant wanted, in a world that had already scorned his need for it, was control.

"You first, then the cat," he told Nora.

Deedee, in typical fashion, appeared annoyed that her agenda was being moved to the back of the line. But Nora looked annoyed, too. It told him a lot about her when she folded her arms over his coat.

Independent. Possibly newly so. No one was going to tell her what to do. Brendan wondered again what the pajamas she was so determined to hide looked like.

"You already told me you aren't a doctor," Nora said.

"Doctor or not, a head injury is nothing to take lightly. They can be sneaky and deadly. It will just take me a minute to look at you."

"I'm fine."

"Deadly?" The boy got a panicky pinched look around his eyes. "Let him look at you!"

Nora, seeing his distress, surrendered, sinking onto a kitchen chair with ill grace.

"That was quite a hit to your head. Do you think you were knocked out?" Brendan moved close, brushed her hair away from the rapidly growing bump.

Every part of her seemed to be either wet or covered with mud. How was it her hair felt like silk?

"I'm fine."

"That's not what I asked," he said mildly.

"I don't think I was knocked out." She offered this grumpily.

"But you can't say for sure?"

She didn't want to admit it, but Brendan could tell she didn't remember, which was probably not a good sign.

Nora knew what date it was, her full name and her birthday. He noted that she was twenty-six, though she looked younger. He also noted, annoyed, that he was interested in her age.

And apparently her marital status. There was no ring on her finger, no signs—large shoes, men's magazines, messes—that would indicate there was any male besides the boy in residence.

Brendan hated that he was awake enough to notice those things, to wonder at her history, what had brought her and her nephew to this remote corner of British Columbia.

Doing his best to detach, he asked more questions. She remembered what had happened right before she was knocked down and right after, though she did not remember precisely what had knocked her down. She could follow the movement of his finger with her eyes.

"You seem fine," he finally decided, but he felt uneasy. A concussion really was nothing to fool around with.

"She is fine," Deedee snapped. "Meanwhile, Charlie could be expiring."

"I'll just have a quick look at the cat," Nora said.

"He's lasted this long. I'm sure he can wait another five minutes. You need to go have a shower and put on something dry."

"Are you always this bossy?"

He ignored her. "If you feel dizzy or if you vomit, or feel like you're going to be sick, you need to tell me right away. Or Luke after I leave. You may have to get to the hospital yet tonight."

She looked as if she was going to protest. And then she glanced down at herself, and surprised him by giving in without a fight.

"All right. Luke, come with me for a minute. You can see if you can find a shirt that will fit Mr. Grant. He's soaked."

That explained her easy acquiescence. She was going to go talk it over with the kid. They were going to get their stories straight and figure out who had done what.

Brendan already knew precisely what she was going to do. She had already started to set it up when she'd said the money had been taken by accident, mistaken for a donation. She was going to take the blame.

Personally, Brendan was strongly leaning toward the conclusion her nephew had done it. How could she possibly think that not letting him accept responsibility was going to do the boy any good?

"Brendan?"

He turned to Deedee, impatient. Was she really going to insist that cat come first again? She did love to have her own way, largely oblivious to the larger picture.

"I'm not feeling well," she said.

He scanned her face. She loved to be the center of attention. But the fear he saw was real.

"My heart's beating too fast," she whispered.

He crossed the room and lifted her frail wrist. Her pulse was going crazy. She searched his face, ready to panic, and he forced himself to smile.

"Let's make it a double header," he said. "We'll take you to the hospital and they can check out Nora at the same time."

He cast Nora a look.

Her protest died on her lips as she read his face and then glanced at Deedee.

"You're right," she said. "I think I need to go to the hospital."

CHAPTER FIVE

AT HIS AUNT'S declaration, panic twisted the boy's features, but only for a second. He took in the situation in the room, his gaze lingering on Deedee. Brendan saw calm come to him, almost as if he had breathed in the truth.

"What about Charlie?" Deedee half whispered, half sobbed. "I can't leave him! Not when he's—"

The steadiness remained in the boy's eyes as he looked to Brendan and then his aunt. "I got the cat," he said, and Deedee relaxed noticeably, slumped against Brendan.

Ninety-two. Deedee could die right now. She could go before the cat. Life liked to put ironic little twists in the story line.

Becky, young and healthy, gone at twenty-six. To this day, it seemed impossible.

A week before she had died, she had said to him, out of the blue, "If I die first, I'll come back and let you know I'm all right."

"You won't be all right," he'd said, uncomfortable with the conversation, pragmatic to a fault. "You'll be dead."

So far, she hadn't been back to let him know anything, even how to keep on living. So he'd been right. Dead was dead.

And he'd been prepared to deal with it tonight with Charlie. Not Deedee. Not on his watch. With a sense of urgency he was trying to disguise, and feeling somewhat like the ringmaster at a three-ring circus, Brendan pulled his cell phone from his pocket and herded all his charges back out the door into the rain.

"Can you get in the back with her?" he asked in an undertone. "Kick my seat if anything changes. You know how to monitor her pulse?"

Nora nodded and climbed in the backseat of the car with Deedee. Luke and the cat got in the front with Brendan. The car smelled of new leather and luxury. It screamed a man who had arrived.

The type of man who would never see anything in the slightly eccentric owner of a struggling animal shelter.

Not that she cared who found her attractive and who didn't! Good grief! The lady beside her could be having a heart attack. This was not the time or place!

Starting the car, Brendan never lost focus. He tucked the phone under his ear. "Hansen Emergency? It's Brendan Grant here. I'm on my way in. I have a ninety-two-year-old woman who has a very fast pulse. No history of heart problems. No chest pain. I also have a young woman who has had a head injury. Who's the doctor on call tonight? I know you're not supposed to tell me, but I want to know."

Nora took it all in. How his name had been recognized, how the name of the on-call doctor had been surrendered to him with a token protest only.

She took in his confidence as he dialed another number. "Greg? Sorry to wake you. Becky's grandmother is not well."

Becky? She'd thought it was *his* grandmother!

"Who's Becky?" she asked Deedee.

"My granddaughter. Brendan's her husband."

Married. Why would that feel the way it did? Like some kind of loss? Why didn't he wear a ring? Nora hated married men who didn't wear rings. They were sneaky, they were looking for—

"She died," Deedee said tiredly.

"I'm so sorry," Nora said, and thought of what she was sure she had seen in his eyes when he'd first leaned over her. The common ground. Now she understood it. Sorrow.

"In a car accident," Deedee went on. She was talking too loudly, the way people who are hard of hearing did. "Brendan doesn't talk about her. I need someone to cry with sometimes. But he never will. He didn't even cry at the funeral."

It was said like an accusation, and so loudly the man in the front seat could not miss it. Nora watched his face in the light coming from the dash. He didn't even flinch. It was as if he was cast in stone.

But she had seen the pain spilling into his eyes in that first unguarded moment when he had stood over her in the paddock.

"People all grieve in their own way," Nora said, and saw him cast her a quick glance in the rearview mirror before he reached for his phone again. "And it seems to me maybe he's there for you in other ways that are just as important."

Not everyone would be chauffeuring an elderly woman and her sick cat around the country in the middle of the night!

"Of course, you're right," Deedee murmured, and leaned her head on Nora's shoulder. Nora had her hand on the woman's wrist and noticed, gratefully, the pulse was slowing to normal.

She listened to the deep gravel of Brendan's voice as he spoke on the phone.

"And I have a head injury, too. I think mild concussion, but a confirmation would be good. See you there. We're five minutes out."

He clicked the phone shut and stepped on the

gas. The night was wet and the roads had to be slippery, but he oozed calm confidence as he navigated the twisty, mist-shrouded road into Hansen. The powerful car responded as if it were a living thing.

The way a man handled a powerful car told you a lot about him. The way a man handled an emergency told you a lot as well. Not that they were tests, but had they been, Brendan Grant would have passed with flying colors.

His calm never flagged. Not on the wet roads, not as they pulled into Emergency, not as he helped his grandmother out of the back of the car. There were obviously benefits to being emotionally shut down.

"What about Charlie?" Deedee wailed again.

"I'll stay with him," Luke said. "Out here. I'm not going in there."

Nora doubted that he was ever going to get over the thing he had about hospitals. He'd spent too much time in one while his mother was sick. He hated them now.

Brendan didn't question why, just flipped a

set of keys at Luke. "Her house is three blocks that way. The address is on the chain. I presume you have your cell phone with you and that your aunt has the number?"

"Why can't I stay here?"

"Because if that cat pees in my car," he said in a low tone that Deedee didn't hear, "it really isn't going to survive the night."

Nora was appalled, but it was a guy thing, because Luke chuckled. Then he sobered. "You're trusting me to go into her house?"

Brendan's eyes locked on his. "Is there any reason I shouldn't?"

Luke ducked his head and didn't say anything.

"I don't know how long we'll be here. Get some rest. Let the cat out of that purse, near his litter box if you can locate it. If your aunt is released, you're going to have to look after her for the rest of the night."

Luke glanced at the address on the key chain. "I hope none of my friends see me with this dorky thing," he muttered, but Nora did not miss the fact that he looked pleased—if some-what guilty—about Brendan's trust.

"I could drive him," she said tentatively, "and come back. I really don't need—"

Brendan gave her a look that was so don't-mess-with-me it made her stomach feel as if it was doing a free fall from ten thousand feet. She just didn't have the energy to take him on.

In the hospital, she had that same sense that you could tell a lot about a man by the way he handled an emergency. Again he passed. He handled the nurse with confidence that was palatable, not the least intimidated by her officiousness. In fact, the exact opposite might have been true. He was obviously well-known in the community, and respected. The nurse treated Brendan as if he was part of that inner circle of the emergency ward.

Interestingly, Vance had been terrible at emergencies. He became so flustered if a badly injured animal was brought in that he could not inspire confidence in anyone. You would have thought with practice he would have gotten better, but he never did. He liked catering to the pudgy poodle set, doing routine checkups and giving shots, neutering, and cleaning teeth.

In fact, he'd opted for regular hours only and hired a young vet to handle the nighttime emergencies, and finally any emergency at all.

A few weeks ago, Nora had heard he was engaged to that young vet. Up until then she had nursed a secret fantasy that he was going to show up on her doorstep, confess the error of his ways and beg her to take him back.

She shook it off. For whatever the reason—she suspected because Brendan Grant made things happen—she found herself ushered into an examination room in record time.

In short order, a young doctor was in, a nurse at his side.

"How's Mrs. Ashton?" Nora asked.

"Old," he said with a resigned smile. "We're going to keep her for observation. So, Brendan says a bump on the head? Maybe knocked out?"

"Maybe," Nora admitted.

"How do you know Brendan?" he asked.

"It's a long story."

The doctor laughed. "That's what he said. He designed our house and supervised the build. He's an amazing architect."

Great! In her weakened state, Nora just had to know Brendan Grant was an all-around phenomenal guy.

The doctor repeated some of the questions Brendan had asked her earlier, shone a light in her eye, got her to follow the movement of his finger.

"I should keep you for observation, too."

"I can't!" she said. "I have animals that will need feeding in—" her eyes flew to a nearby clock "—two hours."

The doctor sighed. "He said you'd say that. I'm going to send you home, but with strict instructions what to watch for. And what to do for the next few hours. Any dizziness, any nausea, any loss of consciousness, you come right back in. I'll give you a handout with symptoms you need to watch for over the next few days. Sometimes even weeks later symptoms can come up."

After having the nurse go over the sheet with her, they let her go. Brendan was in the waiting room.

"You didn't have to wait."

"Uh-huh. How were you going to get home? And collect your nephew?"

"Taxi, I guess."

"And would the taxi driver be watching you for signs of concussion?" Brendan held up duplicates of the instructions the doctor had given her.

The truth was she was glad she did not have to worry about a taxi right now, or how to find Luke. She was glad this man was in charge. And she might have a concussion, so it was okay to be weak. Just this once. Just for tonight.

The animals needed to be fed in a few hours.

She felt like weeping.

Brendan was watching her closely.

"Are you okay?"

"Yes," she said firmly.

But just as if he hadn't heard her, he slipped his arm around her waist, and just as if she hadn't claimed she was okay, she leaned heavily into him.

They collected Luke and, since no one had any idea when Deedee would be home, recaptured Charlie. Nora tried to stay awake and couldn't. She awoke to find herself in Brendan Grant's arms for the second time that night.

There was absolutely no fight left in her.

None.

Because Luke was bringing Charlie into the house instead of out to the barn. She didn't allow any of the animals in the house. How could she? If she did, soon they would be overrun!

But she just didn't have the energy to make a fuss about it right now. Instead, she snuggled deep into Brendan's reassuring strength and let him carry her into her house and up the stairs to her room.

"Is she okay?" Luke asked, pointing Brendan to a room on the right of a narrow hallway. He disappeared with Charlie and the cat carrier into a doorway farther up the hall.

"She's just done in," Brendan assured him. He nudged open the door and hesitated on the threshold of Nora's room.

It was confirmed she was completely, one hundred percent single. No man could be trusted with so much white: white walls, white curtains, white pillows, white bedspread. Her room reminded him of innocence. There was something alarmingly bridal about it.

And that was the last thing Brendan wanted to be thinking of as he carried Nora Anderson across the threshold!

He looked down at her and felt a wave of relief. Still wrapped in his too large jacket, mud from head to toe, she was the world's least likely bride. In fact, her bridal vision of a room was about to be damaged by her muddy little self.

Brendan took a deep breath, stepped in, and quickly made his way to the bed, where he set her on the edge.

Luke appeared in the doorway. "Anything I can do?"

"Oh, Luke," Nora said. "Where did he come from? You know the rules. We can't have animals in the house."

Brendan turned, expecting to see Luke had Charlie. Instead, he had a black-and-white kitten riding in the palm of his hand.

"This one's different," Luke said. "I'm calling him Ranger."

"We don't name them!"

Luke looked mutinous. "I'm keeping him. For my own."

Nora chewed her lip. "We need to talk about that," she said.

"But not tonight," Brendan said firmly. "Luke, can you get rid of the kitten for now, and find me a flashlight?"

He disappeared and came back, with no kitten, but a flashlight.

"Shine it right in your aunt's eyes. Do you see what it does to her pupils? That's called dilation. It's very important that both her pupils are dilating in the same way. I need you to try it."

The boy grasped the flashlight without any hesitation. Brendan was going to take it as a good sign that Luke was not nearly as rebellious as his aunt was.

"Yes, her eyes are doing the same thing. The black part is getting smaller when I hold the light up."

"Don't talk about me like I'm not here!"

"Good. That's exactly what you are looking for. You need to wake her up every hour after I leave and check her eyes. If you see a change you need to call 9-1-1."

"There's no need to frighten him!" Nora protested.

"I'm not frightening him. I'm asking him to step up to the plate. I'm treating him like a man."

Luke puffed up a bit at that.

"Well, he's not a man."

And then deflated.

"He's not a child, either."

The boy puffed up again.

"Either he checks you or I stay for the night."

She blanched at that, then folded her arms over her chest with ill grace and glared at him. That settled, Brendan conducted some very simple tests on his unwilling patient while Luke watched.

"The doctor already did this."

"Luke needs to see what to do."

Finally, Brendan was satisfied. "Do you need anything? A drink of warm milk, maybe?"

"Oh."

There was something kind of sweet and kind of sad about her surprise that anyone would look after her.

"That would be nice," she said shyly.

"Luke, can you go warm some milk?"

Luke left and Brendan leaned over and pulled off her shoes. Gently, he tugged the jacket off her.

"I can do it!"

"It's not as if you're in a see-through negligee."

She scowled at him, but let him free each of her limbs from the jacket.

He pretended not to notice her pajama top at all, but it was adorable. How was it a pink pajama top with kittens on it that said Purrfectly Purrfect Me could be more sexy than a negligee?

"Stand up for a minute," he ordered. She did, and he deftly pulled back the white quilt. Surprise, surprise, pure white sheets.

He guided her under the covers. She sank into her bed, then struggled to sit up. "Set the alarm. I have to be up. I have to feed the animals in two hours."

The clock was holding down some papers on a bedside table. He could tell now wouldn't be the best time to relate what the doctor had told him. She had to rest. Completely. For at least twenty-four hours. She wasn't even supposed to look at a computer screen or read. So he pretended to set the clock.

He looked back at the bed, and her eyes were

already closed, her breath coming out in soft puffs.

So much for the warm milk.

He went and looked at her. He felt the oddest desire to kiss her, not passionately, but a good-night kiss, like a father might give a child. Protective. Happy she was safe.

Happy he had managed to keep at least one person safe from the perils of life.

Brendan went down the steps. The kitchen was empty; no milk was out or on the stove. Luke was stretched out on the living room couch.

The empty carrier was beside him, and Charlie, a cat who hated both animal and man equally, was stretched out over the boy's chest. The black-and-white kitten, Ranger, was curled into Charlie's belly. They were all fast asleep.

Brendan moved closer. Charlie didn't even look like the same cat. He certainly didn't sound like it. The death rattle Brendan had heard earlier was gone.

Maybe he had died. Brendan reached out uneasily and touched him. The cat's fur was warm beneath his fingertips and the animal sighed.

He yanked his hand back. There was no such thing as a healer, he told himself, annoyed. Nora had barely glanced at the cat, anyway.

The boy's cell phone was on the coffee table, and Brendan picked it up and checked. Sure enough, Luke had set the alarm to go off every hour on the hour. But the boy couldn't be trusted to cook milk. Besides, he looked exhausted, with dark circles under his eyes, his face pale and taut, even in sleep.

Brendan suddenly knew he couldn't leave them alone with this.

He could feel it. Around the boy. And around her. They'd both been carrying it for too long.

Brendan flicked through the settings on the phone, turned off the alarm and slowly climbed back up the stairs to Nora's room.

CHAPTER SIX

OUTSIDE THE DOOR of that terrifyingly bridal bedroom, Brendan flicked open his own cell phone.

Logically, he knew he could not take this on right now. He had a deadline coming up. Village on the Lake was an amazing opportunity, and he knew the condo project would be the most prestigious of his career to date.

But once before he had chosen work when there was another choice to be made. He had been driven by his need to succeed, driven to outrun the ghosts of his own childhood, driven to be worthy of a wife who came from far different circumstances than he had.

He had needed to be something, or prove something, to have something he didn't have, and he had made a choice that had left him with nothing at all.

That choice had left his heart trapped behind a wall, in a yawning cavern of emptiness.

Could you come to the same fork in the road again? And make a different choice? Not one that would change what had been, nor could alter what had already transpired, but one that changed who you could be?

He shook off the thoughts, finished dialing. His secretary's voice came over the answering machine.

"You've reached Grant Architects. We can't take your call right now, but we'll get back to you as soon as we can."

"Linda, I won't be in today." Added to all the work that Nora and her nephew undoubtedly did themselves, Deedee was in the hospital. She would need company. And word-search books and updates on Charlie. Brendan had no doubt she would be the world's most impatient patient.

"There is a possibility—" horrible as it was, he recognized it was a real possibility "—that

I might not be in this week. Send—" he named a junior architect "—to supervise the Village."

And then he closed his cell phone and contemplated the magnitude of what he had just done. He didn't miss work. Not ever.

And then, anticipating it would start ringing right at seven—with fires to be put out, clients, construction site foremen, Linda protesting time off was impossible—he shut it completely off.

He knew there were going to be a lot of questions about his absence. Saying it was uncharacteristic was an understatement.

There were going to be a lot of questions.

And he was not at all sure he had any answers. Because niggling at the back of his mind was the thought that he didn't want to be there when they broke ground on Village on the Lake. He didn't want to be there as his plan took on life. He already knew that his feeling of dissatisfaction would grow in proportion to the buildings taking shape, becoming more and more real.

He slid through the door of the bedroom. There was a chair—white, of course—beside her bed and he took it, a bit guiltily, because his clothes were a little the worse for wear also. He was tempted to put his cell phone back on to use the alarm, just as Luke had intended to do.

And then Brendan was annoyed with himself that he had lasted less than a minute without wanting to rely on his cell phone, so stubbornly didn't turn it back on.

It was part of that relentless busyness that had helped him survive. Just like putting even more ungodly hours in at work than he had before the accident.

Something in him *wanted* to stop. That astounded him. Something in him wanted to rest, and be introspective.

Was part of him ready to heal, to crawl back into the light, shielding his eyes from the brilliance? And maybe, just maybe, was this a place where things like that happened? Where something that was dead in a man could be resurrected?

Maybe it was. Look at that cat down there.

Honestly, Brendan could not believe he was

entertaining such thoughts—totally unfounded in any kind of science, totally whimsical, the magical thinking of a little boy.

Mommy, I'm going to buy you a castle some-day. I promise.

The memory of those words shook him, and he shivered as though someone had walked across his grave. Hadn't he known from the minute he had driven under that sign that things were about to go sideways?

Annoyed with himself, he sought refuge in the way he always had, but on a point of pride would not turn on his phone to check the weather or the stock report. He prowled rest-lessly. Starting with the virginal whiteness, the room told him things about her that she might have preferred he didn't know.

There was a picture of her and Luke on her dresser. But none of a man. There was a stack of bills there, too. Why would she have those in her room, unless she wanted to worry over them in private, protect the boy from anxiety?

There was a laundry basket on the floor, full

of neatly folded items. She would have been devastated that her underwear was on top. It reminded him of her pajamas, utilitarian, not sexy. There was no jewelry on the dresser, no nod to that feminine longing for the pretty and the frivolous.

If he was a man who felt things, he might have felt a little sad for her and what the room told him about her. Snowed under with responsibility, alone, and sworn off the small pleasure of celebrating her own prettiness.

And then his eyes went to the papers stuck under the alarm clock. They looked like letters, and he shifted over and cut his eyes to them. He wasn't going to read personal mail.

Only they didn't look personal. In fact, the letter on top began "Dear Rover."

Intrigued, remembering Deedee had said something about Nora being *Ask Rover,* he picked up the letter.

"Dear Rover," he read, "I have a new boy-friend. He is everything I ever dreamed of. Handsome. Funny. He has a good job. There is only one problem. I have a thirteen-year-old malamute cross named Sigh. They hate each other. What should I do?" It was signed "Confused."

The handwriting changed. Though still feminine, it was Rover's—make that Nora's—response, Brendan realized. Further intrigued, he saw she had answered and then crossed it all out. He took the chair next to the bed and squinted to read through the scribbles.

Dear Confused,

Though dogs are capable of such emotions as jealousy, quite often they are better judges of character than human beings. What effort has your prince made to win over your dog? Has your new love been sensitive to the fact your dog is aging, and you might have to soon say good-bye? Has he done one single thing to make that moment easier for you? I'm afraid, from a dog's point of view, he sounds like a jerk. I think you would be better off without him. I am not sure I could be trusted not to bite him, possibly in a place that would make it difficult for him to reproduce. Thank you for your question, though really questions where the answers are of such a life-altering nature might be better answered by your best friend, your mother or your priest. Best barks, Rover.

This was crossed out, but it seemed to him with a certain reluctance.

Brendan felt his lips twitching. He flipped to the next page.

Dear Confused,
Thirteen is very old for a malamute. Do you want to make such a weighty decision based on a dog who will not be with you much longer?

This, too, had been crossed out.

He flipped the page, looking for her answer, but instead found a different letter.

Dear Rover,
My dog, an English bulldog named Petunia, won't come in the basement laundry room. She sits outside the door and howls and shakes. Do you think I have a ghost?
—Haunted

Again, there were two replies. The first, with a big X through it, said:

Dear Haunted,
English bulldogs are known for many lovely traits, intelligence not being among those. Your laundry room is unlikely to be haunted so much as presenting a myriad of smells and sounds beyond poor Petunia's ability to comprehend them. This situation is unlikely to ever get better, so you could save yourself a great deal of frustration by leaving Petunia upstairs while you go to the basement to do laundry. If you give her a chew bone before you go, there is a good chance she won't notice you are gone until you get back.

The second response was measured, and made no comments about the intelligence of bulldogs. It explained that laundry rooms had strange sounds and smells, that Petunia needed to be introduced to the elements separately and slowly, and that dog treats would help.

Still smiling, Brendan set the papers back on the table.

It penetrated his exhaustion that something was different than when he'd arrived.

For a moment he couldn't figure out what it was.

And then he did: it was absolutely quiet. He got up and went to the window. It wasn't just that night was melting into daybreak. The rain had stopped. And on the horizon was something he hadn't seen for forty days and forty nights.

He blinked like a man emerging from a cave.

Or maybe he hadn't seen it since the night his wife and his unborn child had died.

On the horizon, the sun was coming up.

* * *

"Hey, sweetheart, what's your name?"

Nora shook herself groggily. She stared up at the man looking at her, felt his hand on her shoulder.

"Not sweetheart," she said, certain it was a dream and closed her eyes.

That hand on her shoulder, a light in her eyes, "what day were you born?" and then wonderful sleep claiming her again.

"Just for a second, follow my finger with your eyes."

Nora awoke with a start. Sunshine splashed across her bed. Sunshine! The warmth of it was a delight.

All night she had had strange dreams that Brendan Grant was in her room, but now she glanced at the chair where she was sure he had sat, and could clearly see it had been but a dream. The chair was empty.

Sunshine! She looked at the clock. It was noon!

"Oh goodness! The animals!" She sat up too

quickly and it made her feel dizzy. She was aware her head hurt, and other parts of her felt bruised.

How was it possible to feel so good, filled with wonderful dreams, and so bad at the same time? Physically aching, sick that she had slept through looking after her animals.

She lay back down, just for a moment.

"Hey."

Brendan Grant was standing in her doorway. Despite the fact he was in the same shirt as last night, and it had been wet, and dried wrinkled, and his hair was rumpled and his face becoming shadowed with whiskers, he looked amazing. Handsome, oozing confidence, one of those superannoying guys who took charge.

Superannoying unless you happened to be in need of someone to take charge!

"Don't sit up. Doctor's orders. You have to rest. All day."

She couldn't let on for a single second that, in her weakened state, she found that take-charge attitude ever so slightly attractive.

"I can't rest all day! I have to look after the animals."

"I've got it covered."

She scowled at him so he would never guess how much those words meant to her.

"You sat with me all night," she said. She knew she should be appreciative. It came out sounding like an accusation.

"I did."

"That's an unexpected kindness to the stranger you think swindled your grandmother."

"I was hoping you'd talk in your sleep."

"Did I?" she asked, aghast.

"What are you afraid of? A confession? Don't you remember? I asked you questions every time I woke you up."

"Yeah, like what my name was. And my birthday."

He slapped himself on the forehead. "Shoot. I didn't take advantage."

For some reason she blushed, as if he meant taking advantage in a different way. He lifted an eyebrow.

"I didn't take advantage like that, either," he said softly.

"I wasn't suggesting you had," she said primly. Feeling terribly vulnerable, she pulled her quilt up around her chin. "If you'll excuse me, I need to get dressed. I need to look after my animals."

"They're all looked after."

"But how?"

"Luke helped."

"Oh," she said uneasily. She didn't really like the thought of Brendan being alone with Luke, interrogating him.

"Don't worry, he didn't tell me a thing."

She didn't like that she was transparent, either!

"Even though I shamelessly tried to pry information out of him."

"About?" she asked, attempting a careless tone.

"I started small, building up to the big question. I asked where you were from, and he said from a nice place, not a dump like this. I asked how long you had been here, and he said too long, and I asked how old he was and he said nineteen."

"We're from Victoria, we've been here six months and he just turned fifteen."

"Then I asked him who took the money from Deedee."

She held her breath.

"He said lots of people open the mail. The place is practically overrun with volunteers. He said he thought some of those old ladies were pretty shifty looking." Brendan was watching her way too closely. "Are they?"

She felt backed into a corner. Of course her volunteers were not shifty looking! But she wasn't calling Luke a liar, either. She fidgeted with the quilt and didn't answer.

"I thought I'd better find out for myself who looked shifty. So I had Luke call some of them to come help with morning chores. Funny, I can't really see any of the ones who showed up stealing from my grandmother, but I interrogated them, anyway."

"You did not," she said skeptically.

"I did. They all admitted to opening mail. None of them looked guilty, though. None of them remembered a letter from my grandmother. Of course, I'm not sure any of them would have remembered what they had for breakfast this morning. Don't you have a system for dealing with mail? It doesn't seem very efficient that anyone who feels like it, or wanders by the mailbox, opens the letters."

"Systems are not my strong suit."

"Neither is volunteer selection. If the ones who showed up today are any indication, it's kind of like having my grandmother for a volunteer. The old biddy brigade."

Now he sounded like Luke!

"They are invaluable to me!" The truth was Nora needed some young, strong people to volunteer, but they just weren't who showed up when she put an ad in the paper. She hated it that the weaknesses in her organization were so blatantly apparent to him after an hour or two.

"But you can't let any of your current volunteers near a large animal. They can't do any heavy work. One's afraid of dogs and one is allergic to cats. They all hate the parrot. Who bites."

"That's Lafayette. Did he bite you?"

"Of course he bit me. Luke says he bites everyone. Before saying things that would make a sailor blush. In three languages."

"Did you put antiseptic on it?"

"Who's looking after who?"

He was gazing at her keenly. She had sounded way too much like she cared. He was a tyrant, obviously. He'd waltzed in here and completely taken over. She couldn't just let him!

"I don't want to get sued. After infection sets in and your finger falls off. Then you sue me, and at your recommendation, I've lose the funding from the Hansen Community Betterment Committee."

"I haven't decided about a recommendation to the HCBC. Yet."

"And please don't alienate all my volunteers."

"I couldn't alienate your volunteers if I tried, and believe me, I did. But oh, no, they came around the barn after me, promising me cookies, brownies and roast beef dinner. And talking about what a nice girl you are. And available. 'What a shame. No boyfriend. And so pretty, too.'"

"I don't have a boyfriend because I don't want one," Nora told him, and felt a crimson blush go up her cheeks.

"Some jerk broke your heart," Brendan said, and his tone was light, but his eyes were not. They darkened with a menace that made her gasp.

He was seeing way too much, and it had to stop!

"Get out of my room. I need to shower and get dressed."

He sighed theatrically. "It's as hard to pry information out of you as it is out of your nephew. Do you need help?"

Her mouth fell open. She gasped like a fish on a bank.

He laughed, backed into the hall, his hands

in cowboy surrender, and shut the door. But he had to get in the last word.

"If you're dizzy or feel like you're going to vomit, call me. Even if you're naked."

CHAPTER SEVEN

NORA WAS GLAD Brendan Grant was on the other side of that door and couldn't see her face. *Even if she was naked?*

He was trying to shock her, and she was not going to give him the satisfaction of responding.

"Especially if you're naked," he called through the door.

So much for not giving him satisfaction. Nora picked up her shoe from where he had pulled it off her foot last night. She hurled it at the door and heard his hoot of pleasure that he had gotten to her.

She looked around her bedroom. Her world felt like a big mess, with chaos everywhere! Even her beautiful Egyptian cotton sheets, one of the things she had treated herself to before she became guardian to a very expensive fifteen-year-old, were dirty. Her sense of messiness increased when she went into the en suite bathroom and saw herself in the mirror.

Her hair, face and clothes were smudged with mud. She looked like a terrible cross between a cast member of *Oliver* and, with the lump rising over her eye, Quasimodo. Luckily, she told herself, she was not in the market for a man, and especially not a man like the one who had totally invaded her world.

Still, it did not feel lucky at all that *that* man was intent on invading her world when she looked like this! Somehow around a guy like that, a woman—any woman, even one newly sworn to fierce independence—wanted to look her best.

She desperately needed these moments to collect herself. The water of the shower was an absolute balm. She told herself it wasn't weakness that made her apply the subtlest hint of makeup. It was an effort to regain some confidence. And hide her bruises. And erase first impressions!

After showering and applying makeup, with

far more care than she would have wanted to admit, Nora chose a flattering shirt, short-sleeved and summery as a nod to the sun finally making an appearance, and designer jeans, remnants of her old life when she'd bought designer things for herself and never worried about money.

She convinced herself the makeover worked. She convinced herself she felt like a new woman.

She felt ready to battle for her independence! Ready to fight any inclination to lean on another!

Brendan was alone in her kitchen. She paused in the darkness of the hallway before he knew she was there.

Despite her vow to be unaffected by him, it was hard not to take advantage of that moment to study him.

There was no doubt about it. Brendan Grant was a devastatingly attractive man with that dark hair and matching eyes, the slashing brows and straight nose and strong chin. He radiated a subtle masculine strength, a confidence in himself that was not in any way changed by the fact he was in a wrinkled shirt or his hair was roughed or the planed hollows of his cheeks were darkening with whiskers.

The annoying fact was her kitchen was improved by a man standing at the counter, supremely comfortable in his own skin, eating cookies.

"Sorry," he said, when he saw her. "I helped myself."

"No, that's good. I should have told you to make yourself at home."

But she was stunned by the longing that statement awakened in her. A man like this making himself at home? The image somehow deepened her definition of home, made it richer and more complex, and filled her with yearning.

She recouped quickly. "Speaking of which, you need to go home. You must be exhausted. And want a shower. And a change of clothes. And don't you need to check on your grandmother?"

"But who is going to make sure you don't do anything you're not supposed to do?"

"Luke will. Where is Luke?"

Brendan nodded toward the living room, and she went and peeked. Luke was sitting on the sofa, feet on the coffee table, head nodding against his chest. Charlie was sprawled out across his belly, kneading, the way contented cats do. The kitten was perched on his shoulder, batting at a strand of his hair, and Luke swatted it as if a fly was bothering him in his sleep.

"If only such cuteness could last," she said ruefully.

Brendan came and stood beside her. She could feel his presence, even though he didn't touch her, energy tingling off him.

"Ditto for Charlie," he said. "It's not as if he's a nice cat. He's waited under Deedee's sofa and attacked my ankles. You think that doesn't make you nervous?"

Brendan chuckled. And so did Nora. It was a small thing. A shared moment of amusement.

It made her need to get rid of him even more urgent.

As if he sensed the danger of the moment as acutely as she had, he frowned. "Charlie seems way better than he was last night. Are you, er, doing something?"

"No. There's nothing to do, I'm afraid. How old is he?"

"Seventeen, I think."

"That's pretty old for a cat," she said carefully.

"I think so, too. Unfortunately, Deedee has a friend whose cat made it to twenty-three."

"I wouldn't tell her Charlie is feeling better," Nora suggested.

She knew it was an opportunity for him to make a crack about her missing an opportunity to get some more money out of Deedee, but he didn't take it.

"Okay, I won't tell her. Though it is obvious, even to me, a tried-and-true cynic, that he is feeling better." He added, "I'm going. Do not do a single thing today. Do you hear me?"

"Are you always so masterful?" she said, raising an eyebrow, unimpressed.

"Why?" he asked softly. "Do you like masterful?"

"No!" She'd better be careful. She didn't have a shoe handy to throw. Instead, she quickly changed tack. "I'll catch up on some of my inside things."

She was giving in just a little, to make him go.

"You're not even supposed to read. Except your symptom sheet, which tells you not to read. And don't use the computer. No answering *Ask Rover*."

She stiffened. "What do you know about *Ask Rover?*"

"There were some letters beside your bed."

"You read my mail!"

"It was lying out. I had to think of a way to stay awake. Sorry." He didn't sound contrite.

She *hated* that he knew.

And then she didn't.

Because he said, "I liked the first response better. The dog knew the guy was a jerk." And

Brendan smiled at her, as if he actually *liked* it that she was *Ask Rover*. "Is that the one you'll use? About biting him where it counts?"

Nora could feel her face getting very red. That had not been meant for anyone to see.

"No," she said, "it won't be."

"That's a shame."

And it sounded as if he meant it!

"I'll be back," he said.

"No!"

That sounded way too vehement.

"You've done enough," she amended hastily. "I'm very appreciative. Really. But I can take it from here."

"Uh-huh," he said, without an ounce of conviction. He gave her one long look, and then patted her shoulder and was gone.

And suddenly she was alone, in a house that was changed in some subtle and irrevocable way because he had spent the night in her bedroom and eaten cookies at her kitchen counter.

And just as she had a secret side that answered letters to *Ask Rover* exactly the way she wanted to, she had a secret side that listened to his car start up and said, *Usually when a man spends the night something a little more exciting happens! Maybe next time.*

"There isn't going to be a next time," she informed her secret side.

But, of course, there was. Because he had said he was coming back, and he did. One of the volunteers must have told him when they did evening chores and feeding, because he was there promptly at seven. Nora peered out the living room window at him getting out of his car.

He was dressed more appropriately, in a plaid jacket, and jeans tucked into rubber boots. Really, the ready-to-grub-out-pens outfit should have made Brendan less attractive. And didn't. At all.

Nora breathed a sigh of relief when he made no move toward the house. Luke, bless his heart, was already at the barns. She was glad to be rid of him, too. He had absolutely hovered all day, Charlie in his arms and Ranger on his heels.

She knew, somehow, she should have insisted

he take the cats with him when he went to do chores, and leave them in the barn, but she hadn't.

Charlie didn't like her, and had retreated under the sofa as soon as Luke left, then slunk off up the stairs, probably to Luke's room. It didn't matter. She didn't have to lay her hands on him to know his life force was leeching out of him. The antics of the kitten entertained her, but didn't occupy her enough for her to outrun her own thoughts.

Which let her know her relief that Brendan had headed for the barns instead of the house was pretended relief. Part of her wanted him to come up here. Which probably explained why she was still in the designer jeans and top, and not her pj's despite a full day of doing nothing.

Unless you counted catching up on movies. She scowled at the TV. Since he'd arrived— since she knew he was out there—she had no idea what was going on in the movie.

Then she heard them coming. She felt like a high school girl waiting for her prom date. She checked her buttons. Ran a hand through her hair. Tried to pull her bangs over the bump on her forehead. She tried to decide how to sit so that it looked as if she was completely surprised and a little bored by the fact Brendan was coming to her house.

Luke let him in, so he didn't knock.

And then he was standing there, filling her space, gazing at her, and her silly heart was beating way too hard.

"How are you feeling?" he asked.

If she told him the truth about her racing pulse, she'd probably be whisked off to the hospital, just as Deedee had been. "Bored."

He looked past her to the TV. "What movie?"

Why hadn't she thought of that when she was preparing to see him again?

She snapped it off. "Something silly. I just turned it on to keep from going crazy."

"Uh-huh."

"It's that pirate one," Luke said, coming back with Charlie. "It's for babies, but she's seen it three times. Because of Johnny Jose." He rolled his eyes disparagingly.

Brendan's lips were twitching as if her crush on Johnny Jose was amusing. "So you're feeling all right? No signs of dizziness? Not feeling sick?"

"I'm fine." If he said uh-huh she was going to scream. Instead he stuck his hands in his pockets and rocked back on his heels and studied her. She tilted her chin defiantly.

"This is cool, Auntie Nora. Brendan gave the old lady a tablet so she can see some video of Charlie while she's in the hospital."

How, exactly, could you steel yourself against something like that?

Or what followed. Luke put down Charlie, got out a piece of string and tied a lump of hay to it. "This is a mouse," he narrated. Then he pulled it across the floor.

The black-and-white kitten exploded across the room after the hay. Luke shouted with laughter. It was the most animated she had seen her nephew in a long, long time. And then he went and dangled the string in front of the couch, where Charlie had retreated.

A ginger paw came out and swatted. Then swatted again. Then both paws shot out, and Charlie grabbed the "mouse" with such strength he pulled it from Luke's hand, yanking it under the couch with him.

Brendan lowered the phone that he had been recording the scene with, and stared at the place where Charlie had disappeared. "That is like the old Charlie," he said uneasily, "the one who likes to attack ankles."

"Did you get it?" Luke asked, then sighed. "Not that Mrs. Ashton will be able to figure out how to open it. Auntie Nora wouldn't be able to."

Why don't you just tell him all my secrets? Crush on Johnny Jose. Computer illiterate. Ask Rover. *He's going to know me better than I know myself if this keeps up.*

Brendan still looked faintly dazed. "I'll go see Deedee and make sure she got it. I can show her on my phone if she didn't figure it out. I'll be back first thing tomorrow for chores."

Nora opened her mouth to protest. First, she didn't think it was a good idea for him to show that footage to Deedee. Second, she didn't think he should come back here.

But she saw Luke's quick look of pleasure before he masked it by snaring the mouse from under the couch and getting Ranger going again.

He liked Brendan. He wanted to believe the cat was getting better. Couldn't she just let life ride, for once?

"Good job with the horses," Brendan said to Luke. "Remember not to let your aunt anywhere near them. And be sure and check her one more night. Can you do that?"

"You had me at the deadly part," Luke said, glancing up from the kitten, and he and Brendan exchanged a grin.

Three days later, Brendan was still showing up to do chores. Nora had started to do a pretty good job of hiding out, which was necessary because chores always finished with Brendan and Luke coming to the house to produce a new video of Charlie. Not only was the aging cat alive and well, but he seemed to be improving.

Deedee was home from the hospital, but confined to bed. She was so impressed with the changes in Charlie she hoped to leave him at Nora's Ark a bit longer.

But enough was enough! Nora was completely recovered. Really, there had been nothing to recover from.

A whole lot of fuss about nothing.

And she'd had enough of hiding out in her own home. It was time to tell Brendan Grant, nicely, that he had to exit her life. Goodbye. Nice meeting you. Get lost. Could he take Deedee's cat home to her at the same time?

Charlie was in the house. Luke was getting way too attached to him—he seemed to like him even more than the kitten—and Nora seemed to be the only one determined to remember that there was going to be no happy ending for the old cat.

It was way too obvious to her that there were

no happy endings, period, and it was a crazy thing to hope for.

She wasn't hiding out today. She was waiting in the living room, her plan firmly in place. She was getting rid of them—the cat and Brendan Grant. And at the same time, she was getting rid of this part of her that wanted so desperately to attach itself to the possibility of happy endings.

She rehearsed from the moment she heard his car. *Thanks so much. Quite capable. Very independent. Lots of volunteers. No room for the cat. Vamoose, both of you.*

And then the door opened, and Luke and Brendan didn't come into her space so much as they spilled into it, like sunshine piercing the dark. Brendan's head was cocked to Luke. She heard his low laugh at something her nephew said.

Her plan faltered.

Brendan Grant was here to help. She wasn't sure if he had intended to help her nephew, but it was certainly a possibility. Look how good he was with his grandmother. Still, whether it had been his intention or not, she saw subtle changes in Luke with this positive daily male influence.

When, she wondered, had she become this woman? So interested in protecting herself that she thought she didn't have to show one speck of gratitude to someone who was helping her. And helping that tiny two-person unit that was her family.

She was Luke's main role model. She had a responsibility. Was that what she wanted to teach him about life? Protect yourself at all costs?

So what if she found Brendan attractive? Surely she could control herself! It would be akin to meeting Johnny. You wouldn't be helpless. You wouldn't throw yourself at him. You wouldn't embarrass yourself or him.

You would act as though your heart was not beating a mile a minute. As though you were a mature woman capable of great grace and confidence.

You would step up to him and look him in the eye. And smile.

"Hi, Brendan," she heard herself say, calm and mature, a woman she could be proud of. "Thanks so much for all your help around here. I really appreciate it."

That would have been good enough. More than good enough.

So why did she have to add, "I made lasagna tonight. There's extra. Do you want some?"

"Aunt Nora makes the best lasagna. Lots of cheese," Luke said, and his hope that Brendan would stay was somehow heartbreaking.

Too late, Nora wondered what she was letting them in for.

Particularly when Brendan said, "It would take a better man than me to turn down home-made lasagna. Especially the kind with lots of cheese."

CHAPTER EIGHT

WHAT THE HELL was he doing? Brendan asked himself as he sat at Nora's table for the second night in a row. Lasagna last night. Meat loaf tonight.

"You wanna stay and play Scrabble?" Luke asked, oh so casually, as if he didn't care what Brendan's answer was.

And out of the corner of his eye he watched Nora, as he always watched Nora, and saw her tensing, caught just as he was between wanting him to go and wanting him to stay.

"Scrabble?" he said. "I'm not staying to play Scrabble."

Luke tried to hide how crestfallen he was. Nora got a pinched look about her mouth and eyes.

It should have confirmed he could not stay

here to play Scrabble. Instead he heard himself saying, "Don't you know how to play poker?"

And when they both shook their heads, he said, "I guess it's about time you learned."

An hour later Luke was rolling on the floor laughing. Brendan's own stomach hurt from laughing so hard. The rock had been rolled away and light was penetrating into every corner of that cave.

He needed to stop. He needed to ponder hard questions. He needed to slow down, roll the rock back in place, regroup, retreat, rethink.

Why was he doing this? The truth? Something in him was watching that damned cat getting better and better. Something in him was surrendering, resisting his efforts to be logical, telling him that if that cat could be healed, maybe he could, too.

Healed from what? he asked himself. Until he had passed under that Nora's Ark sign, hadn't he been blissfully unaware of his afflictions?

No, that wasn't true. There hadn't been one blissful thing about his life. It had been cold and dark and dank and gray. Certainly there had been no moments of laughter like this.

He had managed to avoid his demons—guilt, dark despair, crippling loneliness—by filling the confines of the space he had chosen with ceaseless work, by never stopping.

He had thought if he stopped he would find his afflictions had run along with him, silent, waiting.

He thought if he ever stopped, those tears that had never been cried would begin to flow, and would flow and flow and flow until he was drowning in them and in his own weakness.

His hardened heart behind its wall, a life that yawned with emotional emptiness, that had protected him.

And now Nora's laughter was lapping against it, like water against a refuge built of mud, lapping away, steadily eroding the defenses.

How could you defend against moments like these?

"You are," he told her, "without a doubt the worst card player I have ever seen. Give that deck to Luke before you mark it so badly I'll own your house."

"What do you mean, mark it?"

Luke took the cards from her. "See this bend you made here? Now everyone knows that's the ace of spades."

"Oh," she said, the only one who didn't know.

And she simply didn't have the face for poker! She frowned at bad hands. She chewed her lip if they were really bad. Her eyes did a glow-in-the-dark thing if it was a good hand.

"Your aunt is a wash-out at this game. You have some promise, though. You have to have some ability to lie to be a good poker player."

Luke flinched as if he'd been struck. He ducked his head. He dealt them each a hand and glared at his. And then he set them down, face up. He cleared his throat and looked Brendan right in the eye.

"I did it," he blurted out. "I opened the mail. I sent Deedee the letter. I took the money."

Honestly, Brendan did not want to like this kid.

But coupled with the defense of his aunt with

the coat rack, and how hard he worked out there in the barn every day, how good he was with that cat and all the animals, the confession meant there was some hope for the boy.

If Nora didn't manage to kill him with kindness first.

Because his aunt put down her cards—a royal flush, not that she would recognize it—and glared at Luke, ready to fight for him, ready to believe in him. "Luke! No, you didn't!"

"Let him do the right thing," Brendan said quietly.

The words made Nora want to weep. It confirmed what she already guiltily believed. She was making the wrong choices for Luke over and over again.

Nora hated that Brendan was right. And she hated that he had come into her house and her life and had taken control as naturally as he breathed.

But most of all, she hated the sense of relief she felt that she didn't have to figure out how to fix it. She hated what it said about her that she had been prepared to lie to protect her nephew. And she hated, too, that she felt the same way she had felt in Brendan's arms. Not so alone. Carried.

"Why don't you tell us what happened?" Brendan suggested.

Nora appreciated his tone. Mild but stern. Not about to take any nonsense.

Luke glanced at her, and she nodded, not missing the look of relief on his face. He'd been carrying the guilt for too long.

"I was opening the mail for Nora's Ark and found Deedee's letter. She didn't say Charlie was dying. She just said he wasn't feeling well. I decided to play along. So I wrote her and said sure I'd send some energy. But that she should make, er, a donation."

"You told her to send money," Brendan said flatly, not willing to allow Luke to sugarcoat it.

"Okay. I did."

"But why? You have money," Nora asked plaintively.

"I didn't have enough."

She felt herself pale. Enough for what? Why did a fifteen-year-old boy need fifty dollars that he couldn't ask her for?

Cigarettes? Alcohol? Drugs?

Karen, I have failed. Colossally. Why did you leave me with this?

Given the road she was going down, at first she thought Luke's answer was a relief.

"The police were hassling me about the bike. The guy I borrowed it from, Gerald Jack-in-the-Box—"

"Jackinox," she corrected automatically, thinking, *It's about the bike. Not drugs.*

"Whatever. He said he'd make it go away if I gave him fifty bucks."

Her sense of relief evaporated. "That's black-mail! Tell me you didn't ask Mrs. Ashton for fifty dollars to give to him! Oh, Luke, why didn't you come to me?"

He at least had the grace to look a little shame-faced. "I asked her for fifty bucks. Cash. In the mail. When the money actually came, I was shocked. And I felt guilty. So I sat down and thought I'd send her stupid cat—I didn't know him then—some energy."

"What do you mean by that?" Brendan asked, his voice stern.

"Well, just the way my aunt does it."

"And what way is that? That your aunt does it?"

"That's not important!" Nora said. Her way with animals had always made her a bit of a novelty—and not always in a good way—to those who knew about it. Brendan Grant already knew way too much about her. He'd guessed she'd been betrayed. He knew she had a secret crush on Johnny Jose. He'd read *Ask Rover* and knew she wrote it. Enough was enough!

But annoyingly, Brendan trumped her with Luke. By a country mile.

"She puts her hands on the animal and then closes her eyes and goes all quiet. So that's what I did. Only I had to pretend the cat was there. I sort of imagined light going around him. It was dumb, because I didn't have a clue what the cat looked like. I didn't picture him being so ugly. I mean, not that he's ugly once you get to know him."

"That's the same with all things, and people, too, Luke," Nora said, not wanting to miss an opportunity to help him see things in a way that would make him a better person.

Luke and Brendan both rolled their eyes.

"Right," Luke muttered. "Anyway, it freaked me out because I got all warm, like the sun came out, and it was pouring rain that day. It freaked me out even more when Mrs. Ashton wrote that it worked, so I just threw out her letter. And erased her messages. Geez, she called about a dozen times a day. I was a wreck trying to get to the answering machine before my aunt."

Nora cast Brendan a glance. He didn't look at all sympathetic to Luke feeling like a wreck trying to keep his treachery hidden.

"Why," Brendan asked carefully, "did it freak you out when you thought it worked? You could have been into some real cash."

"I didn't like the way it felt."

Nora's sweet sensation of relief was tempered somewhat when Luke shrugged and sent her a look. "Who wants to be like her?"

Even though she was used to his barbs, it hurt. And even though it was the story of her life. She was careful not to let how badly it hurt show.

Over the years, some people saw what she did as a gift, but most saw it as just plain weird. She was cautious about showing people that side of herself. Even in the column, she didn't reveal she wrote it, didn't always say exactly what she wanted to say, tempering it with what people wanted to hear.

Nora glanced at Brendan. He was watching her. She had the uneasy feeling he saw everything, even the things she least wanted to reveal.

Again she had that aggravating feeling. Instead of feeling exposed, she felt in some way not alone.

She tore her eyes away from him, forced herself to focus on her nephew. "Luke, do you understand how terrible this is? You gave false hope to a poor little old lady—"

"No one would resent being called old more than Deedee," Brendan said mildly, "and we won't even go into the poor part."

"The point is she was afraid to lose her cat, and Luke played on her fear and took her money."

"I needed the fifty bucks!"

"You allowed that boy to blackmail you! I have to call his parents."

"That's why I didn't tell you! Dammit, Auntie, I didn't really have permission to borrow his bike. Do you have to be so gullible?"

Brendan's tone remained mild enough, but there was steel running through it. "You don't use language like that in front of women. And your aunt is not the guilty party here. You are. What really happened with the bike?"

Nora was aware she should have said that, not him. She felt it again, though. The tempting weakness of liking the fact she was not handling this alone.

"I took it," Luke said, jutting out his chin defiantly. "I stole Gerald's bike because he was mean to me. He made fun of my hair in front of the whole class. You think it's not hard enough being new? And everybody knowing your aunt does voodoo?"

"Voodoo," Brendan said, with just a trace of approval.

"What do you mean, everybody knows I do voodoo?" Nora asked, horrified. "I don't! I run a shelter for abused and abandoned animals. That's all!"

"No, it isn't," Luke said wearily.

And suddenly she wondered if it had been about Luke's hair at all. Or if it had been about her.

"Anyway," Luke continued, "Gerald said he'd back my story that I borrowed the bike if I gave him fifty dollars."

"You've made everything worse," Nora said, but not too strongly. It was bad enough Luke was being teased about his hair. He was being teased about her, too! She was an adult and she could barely handle the mockery. That was why she wrote her column in secret.

"I think the question now is how are you going to fix all this?" Brendan asked.

"Naturally, we'll give your grandmother back her money," Nora said, hearing the resignation in her voice.

"No. *You* won't," Brendan said.

"Excuse me?"

"Luke did it. He needs to figure out how to make amends to her."

"What's amends?" Luke asked suspiciously.

"Just what it sounds like. You broke something, you mend it."

He pondered that. "I don't know how."

"I'll give you a chance to figure it out."

Luke seemed to be back to his old self, arms folded over his narrow chest, bristling with barely contained hostility.

Take charge, Nora ordered herself, so she added, "Figure it out. With no computer. And no cell phone."

"That sucks," the boy said, and got up from the table and marched away.

"You're bossy," Nora said to Brendan, feeling somehow she had to hide the fact that she was so grateful someone was helping her through this.

"You've already said that."

"Sorry to bore you by repeating myself." She needed time to gather herself. Needed to show leadership, and wasn't. She was letting Brendan take charge.

Only because it had been a strange week. She'd been injured. She'd let down her guard around Brendan. Invited him into her life.

Still, it was a new blow that Luke was being teased at school because of her.

"Tell me what you've heard about me," she said to Brendan.

"Deedee heard you were a healer. She was making biblical references, about the laying on of hands. She's expecting a miracle."

Nora groaned softly. "I'm sorry. Do you think

that's what Luke's classmates are hearing about me, too?"

"I assume some version of that. You bring a dead dog to life, and you're the talk of the town."

"I didn't bring a dead dog to life!"

"You're not used to small towns, are you?"

"No."

"It's like that game you played in junior high school. The teacher whispers, 'The green tree on Main Street is dying,' to the first kid in the line, and they whisper it to the next. But twenty kids later it has become 'Mrs. Green killed her husband on Main Street with a tree branch.'"

"We never played a game like that in school."

"A shame. The power of distortion would not be such a surprise to you. What really happened with the dog?"

"He'd been hit by a car. He was knocked out. Not dead."

"Technicalities. So, you have no gift with animals?"

"I didn't say that. I've always liked animals,

sometimes a whole lot more than people. There is an energy element to animals that is very strong, and I seem to be able to connect with that. But I'm not a vet, and I don't try to take the place of one."

"Ah."

She had said enough. But despite her vow to herself to keep the barriers up between her and Brendan, it felt strangely and nicely intimate to be sharing her kitchen with him, telling him things she didn't always feel free to say.

"What I have no gift with, I'm afraid, is adolescent boys," she added, since she seemed bent on confessing private things about herself.

"I see cookies in a jar and good food on the table every night. There are drawings on the fridge and homework being done. Where are his folks?"

She could not quite keep the shaking from her voice. "My sister died."

"And his dad?"

"He went before Karen. Luke's never said

anything to you? You guys have been doing chores together for days."

"Yeah, well, you know guys."

But she didn't. She didn't know guys at all. That was probably part of the problem with Luke.

Brendan sighed. "We don't talk about *deep* things. Discussion runs to who is the best hockey player in the world. Last night's baseball scores. Who can clean a cat cage the fastest and with the least gagging."

Nora really didn't want to confide one more thing to this man. But she heard herself saying, "I'm not sure that Karen would have trusted me by myself with this. She saw my fiancé, Vance, as the stable one, a vet with a well-established practice. I'm afraid I've always been seen as the family black sheep."

"It seems to me your sister would think you were doing well at making a home for your nephew."

"So, now you know! I'm an orphan," Luke exclaimed from the doorway. "Doesn't that just suck? Who even knew there was such a thing anymore?"

Nora hadn't seen him reappear, but there he was, bristling defensively.

"And you think that isn't bad enough?" Luke continued, jerking his head toward her. "She was going to get married. And then Vance wouldn't marry her. Because of me."

CHAPTER NINE

NORA'S MOUTH FELL open. Her eyes clouded with tears. She'd had no idea Luke knew about that awful conversation between her and Vance.

"Just because I glued his stupid golf clubs to his golf bag."

"Why'd you do that?" Brendan asked mildly.

"He didn't want Auntie Nora to get me a skateboard, because I'd been suspended from school. So she didn't. So I glued his golf clubs to his bag. Super Duper Gobby Glue works just the way it says in the commercial."

"I'll remember that," Brendan promised.

"'It's him or it's me,'" Luke quoted. His mimicry of Vance might have been hilariously accurate, if it wasn't for the context. "She picked me. Dumb, huh?"

And then Brendan said, his voice steady as a rock, "I don't think it's so dumb."

Despite the fact Nora could have done without her whole life story being exposed, she could have kissed Brendan, she felt so grateful.

Unfortunately, that made her look at his lips.

The thought of kissing Brendan Grant made her dizzier than the bump on her head.

"You don't think it was dumb that she picked me?" Luke said, and the hopeful look in his eyes tugged at her heartstrings. He quickly covered it. "Sure. I just took money from your grandmother."

"You know everybody makes mistakes. Your aunt Nora when she got engaged to a jerk."

Her heart filled with the most unreasonable gratitude that someone saw Vance's defection as a statement about him, not about her.

"He was a jerk," Luke said. "A sanctimonious, know-it-all, stuck-up jerk."

Nora's mouth fell open. First of all, she'd had no idea Luke's dislike of Vance had run so deep.

Second, she had no idea that he could use a word like *sanctimonious* correctly.

"She should have asked Rover," Brendan deadpanned, and then he and Luke cracked up. Brendan must have caught her disapproving expression, because he sobered.

"So, everybody makes mistakes," he said. "When you took that money from Deedee, it was a mistake. What matters is whether you choose to grow from them or not."

"What kind of mistakes have you ever made?" Luke challenged, not laughing anymore. Nora could tell he wanted to believe there was hope that a mistake could turn out okay, and was afraid to believe at the very same time.

Which she understood perfectly, of course.

Brendan hesitated. He tossed his cards down on the table. For a moment, it looked as if he wasn't going to say anything at all.

Then, his voice so soft she felt herself straining to hear it, he said, "My wife died because of a terrible mistake I made. She was carrying our baby."

Nora laid her hand on his, almost unbearably grateful that Brendan had seen how great Luke's need was. And possibly hers. That he had overcome so tremendous an inner obstacle and given something of himself to both of them confirmed that her instincts had been right, after all.

There was a common place between them.

But it seemed to her that common place was the most frightening thing of all. It asked her to put aside her past injuries and her petty fears. It asked her to think less about protecting herself and more about reaching out to another human being.

Reaching out to animals was easy. Human beings were far more complicated.

She wasn't ready. She ordered herself to withdraw her hand.

And yet her hand, as if separate from her mind and linked to her soul, stayed right where it was.

Brendan could not believe he had said that to Nora and Luke. What if these were the words that broke open that dam of emotion within him?

But no, the dam was safe. He had not cried then, and he would not cry now. Still, there was nothing he hated more than sympathy. He waited for her to say something that would make him regret confiding in them even more than he already did.

But Nora said nothing at all. Instead, with a tenderness so exquisite if felt as if the dam of emotion was newly threatened, she laid her hand on top of his.

For a moment he felt only the connection, her small hand covering part of his larger one, the softness of her palm against his toughened skin.

But then he was stunned by the warmth that began to pour from her hand, some energy vibrating up his wrist into his arm. It felt as if his whole body was beginning to tingle.

And suddenly, the world's greatest cynic believed what he had only suspected until now.

She could heal things.

The light shining in her eyes almost made

him believe she could heal the most impossible thing of all: a heart smashed to pieces.

For a stunned second, he felt his throat close. But then he fought it.

Because who would want that fixed? For what reason? So that it could be smashed again? So that a man could face his impotency over the caprice of life all over again?

He jerked his hand out of hers, and she stiffened, guessing it, correctly, as rejection. Then she had the good sense to look relieved. She actually glared at her hand for a minute, as if it had mutinied and acted on its own accord.

She turned rapidly from him, ran a hand over her eyes, winced when she touched the bump on her head.

"I should get some footage of Charlie for Deedee and then go," he said.

Luke, looking pensive and solemn, went and got the cat.

Nora was completely composed when she turned back to Brendan.

"Thank you for telling us. I know it was hard

for you. And yet he needed to hear it. He's known you only a short time, but he looks up to you."

Brendan shrugged, withdrawing, uncomfortable.

Luke came back with Charlie and set him on the counter.

The cat gave a yowl of indignation and made for the edge, as if he fully planned to leap to the floor.

Brendan stared. This was a cat that had barely been able to lift his head a few days ago. "What are you feeding him?"

Luke made a quick grab and caught Charlie by the back of the neck. The cat hunkered down, resigned but unhappy.

"There's no cure for old age," Nora told Brendan gently. "There's nothing that stops life from unfolding in its natural order."

As Luke lifted his other hand so that both of them rested on the cat, Brendan was aware again of that vibration, of an energy he didn't understand. It was almost as if the light in the room changed.

The cat stopped struggling. It was as if Charlie had been tranquilized. He closed his eyes and a deep purr came from him.

Luke jerked his hands away. He took the cat off the counter, set him on the floor, watched him scoot off. Uncaring that there would be no pictures tonight, he shoved both hands in his pockets. His face was white and his voice was brimming with anger.

"Life's natural order?" he spat out. "My mom was thirty-four. What's natural about that? Oh, and Aunt Nora is a healer, all right. Ask anyone. My mom always talked about my auntie Kookie, how her room was filled with mice and birds and cats and dogs, and she could heal them all."

"Luke, that's an exaggeration. I liked animals. I couldn't—"

But he cut her off. "I was here when they brought that dog in. It was dead."

"It wasn't," Nora said. "Obviously it wasn't."

"And then she puts her hands on it, and *poof,* he's alive and wagging his tail. And in three days he's running around the yard, bringing me sticks to throw.

"But when it really counts? When it's cancer? Forget it! Who would want a gift like that, anyway? That's why I don't want to be like her! You can't change anything that matters."

And then he spun on his heel and followed the cat, and Nora and Brendan stood in frozen silence as he thumped up the stairs.

"How did he know Charlie has cancer?" Brendan asked.

"He doesn't," Nora said too quickly, her troubled eyes on the empty doorway her nephew had gone through. "His mom—my sister—died of cancer. I'm sorry, I don't think there's anything more I can do for Charlie. You should take him home to Deedee. She can spend his last days with him."

Brendan could feel weariness like a dull ache in his bones.

Not just because it was late, either.

It was the weariness of it all.

A boy who had lost everything and who already knew you could not change anything that really mattered. A woman who was trying desperately to help him through it, even though she had lost, too.

Brendan realized he had actually been thinking that cat was getting better. Had been bringing Deedee pictures, instead of preparing her to face yet another loss.

This was the truth he had been doing his best to outrun for two and a half years. It was just as Luke had said. When it really counted?

A man was powerless.

And there was no feeling in the world quite as bad as that one.

Luke came back down the stairs. He looked as if he had been crying, and Brendan almost envied him those tears, the release they brought from the inner storm.

The boy's face was white and strained with the manful effort of trying not to let everything he was feeling show. He had Charlie tucked under his arm, an unwilling football.

"I'm going to fix him! And I'm going to pay you back your money, too!" Luke stomped back up the stairs.

Nora bit her lip, sent Brendan an imploring look.

He shrugged. He wanted to be a dyed-in-the-wool cynic, but the past few days had challenged that. The aunt had something. He had felt it when she'd touched his arm.

And Luke had something, too. That cat was acting better, even if he wasn't actually getting better.

Though that something that Nora and Luke had—that gift with things wounded—was not necessarily what they needed.

Despite the shrug, he knew his indifference was pretended. Caring had crept up on him.

Brendan recognized their lives were a web he could get tangled in.

Was already tangled in, whether he wanted to be or not. And he didn't want it. He'd spent a long time locked in his lonely place, avoiding entanglement.

He walked out the door, refusing to look back at Nora. Free of the enchantment of her house, walking through the warmth of the early summer evening to his car, Brendan Grant vowed to himself he wasn't coming back here. Not until it was time to pick up Charlie.

Dead or alive.

Nora loved the barn. It had taken a dozen volunteers and a hundred man-hours to make the falling-down old structure into an animal shelter, but now it was perfect. She was in the small-animal section, two rows of roomy cages facing a sparkling clean center aisle.

After a night like last night, she needed the peace she felt working alone here. She had a rock-and-roll station blasting, music from the fifties. It was partly to keep her moving through the exhaustion after twenty-four hours of being woken every hour on the hour. It was partly a nice distraction from her whirling thoughts.

But the animals loved music. Humming along, she reached inside the rabbit cage, picked up a droopy-eared bunny she had named Valentine, and tucked him into her bosom.

He wriggled against her, snuggling deeper.

"You want to dance, sweetheart?"

"Sure."

She whirled. Brendan was standing there, watching her. The rabbit must have taken the sudden hard beating of her heart as a warning of imminent danger, because he scrambled out of her arms, over her shoulder and down her back. He hit the floor running.

Brendan reached behind him and closed the door to prevent bunny escape, then turned back to her.

How unfair that he looked even better in the pure afternoon sunshine streaming through the windows high up the walls than he had looked last night.

He must have come from work. He had on a white shirt and gray pants. A tie was loosely knotted at his throat. He looked handsome and sure of himself, a model for *GQ,* only more real.

And she still had a lump the size of a baseball on her forehead, and was wearing a charming blue smock of the one-size-fits-all variety that swam around her.

"I—I haven't seen you for a few days," she stammered. She hoped there was nothing in her voice that revealed how she had waited. And watched.

And hated herself for both.

"Busy at work," he said.

"What are you doing here now?"

"Deedee insisted. Luke's been sending her pictures, but she had to come see for herself."

Nora had no idea Luke had been sending on pictures of the cat. She probably would have asked him to stop, if she knew. What did they all think was going to happen?

"Yesterday he sent a video of that old cat playing with a ball."

She looked closely at Brendan. "Please tell

me you don't believe that animal is going to get better?"

He shrugged. "I don't know what to believe, Nora. The thing is, *I'm* getting better. And I never believed that would happen."

"What do you mean, better?" she whispered.

He rolled his shoulders. "I've been in total darkness. I can feel the light trying to get through. There are cracks in the wall and light is seeping in, and every time I patch one crack, another one appears."

It felt as if she couldn't breathe. As if she was going to cry. It felt as if she could run to him and put her arms around him and whisper him home.

To her.

"But the walls have become who I am, so when they crumble, will I crumble, too?"

"No," she whispered. "You won't."

"Uh-huh."

The feelings were too strong. To hide how totally vulnerable she felt, Nora got down on her hands and knees and looked under a set of cages. Valentine stared back at her.

And then Brendan was on the floor beside her. His scent, clean and masculine, overrode every other smell in the building. It was not lightening the mood, having him so near, though he, too, seemed to want to back off from the intensity of the previous moment.

"I think he stuck his tongue out at me," he said.

"Like life," she said. "When you most want control, it will stick its tongue out at you."

"Oh boy," Brendan muttered, "I can see it coming now. *Ask Valentine.*"

She laughed and he smiled.

"There he is." He reached under the row of cages; his shoulder brushed hers; Valentine hopped away.

Nora shot back before she did something really dumb, something she would regret forever, and crawled along the floor. "Valentine," she crooned, "come here."

"I dropped Deedee off at the house. Luke said you were down here."

Did that mean Brendan *wanted* to see her? She glanced sideways at him, just as he shoved himself under the bank of cages.

"You're ruining your clothes," she said.

He ignored her. "I'm being outsmarted by a rabbit."

Valentine hopped from underneath and took off down the row.

Brendan crawled out, dusted himself off, stood up. "Can't you call him back with your energy?"

She glanced at him, annoyed at the barb, and then saw the little smile playing across his face. He was teasing her. Something dangerous rippled down her spine.

The awareness of him shivered more intensely around her. It was nice to be teased by him.

For a moment, she was going to fight it. The intensity, the subtle invitation to bring him into the light.

And then she found she couldn't. By his own

admission he had been in darkness. By his own admission he had come here to her.

With an inner sigh of surrender, Nora decided to play. To be the one thing she never was. Totally herself. She had been so serious for so long. She could not resist the temptations of this moment.

CHAPTER TEN

NORA PLACED HER fingers on her temples, squinched her eyes shut tightly and hummed. "Uzzy, wuzzy, fuzzy bunny, let this poem call you home."

She opened one eye when she heard Brendan snicker. "Is it working?"

"That is the worst spell I've ever heard."

"Oh," she said, widening her eyes innocently. "Have you heard many?"

"Thankfully, no."

"Why don't you try?"

He seemed to debate for a moment. Why did her heart begin to beat faster when he gave in to it, too? To the invitation of life not being so serious. A smile tugged at the corners of that sinful mouth.

"How about a carrot instead of an incantation?" he suggested.

"If he was starving, we might have a hope. As you know, since you've been doing it, he's quite well fed. Still…" she went to the fridge at the end of the aisle, removed a bag and handed Brendan a carrot "…we can try. If it doesn't work today, it might work by midweek."

They went back down the aisle, her on one side, him on the other, peering under cages.

"Now that Deedee's feeling better, is she going to make a decision? Is she going to take Charlie home? Or to the vet?" Nora asked.

"She has her own ideas, as always, none of which involve relieving you of Charlie. She seems to have come for a visit. Luke and she were in deep conversation when I left."

"Luke and Deedee? Seriously?"

"Seriously. Hey! Here he is! Here bunny, bunny, bunny." Brendan was down on his knees again, peering under a sink. As she watched, reluctantly enchanted by a man willing to wreck a thousand-dollar suit for a rabbit, he held out the carrot in the palm of his hand. Valentine edged toward him, he made a move to grab him and the bunny leaped sideways and hopped away.

"He's waving his tail at me. Like a middle finger. Wow. Even I can read his energy."

Nora giggled. Brendan turned and glared at her, but a smile lurked in his eyes. "Let's see if he'll fall for the bait again."

Really, she knew if they left the rabbit alone, he'd eventually get hungry and come out. But it was too fun trying to catch him with Brendan.

Together they chased that bunny all over the barn, acting silly, making faces, doing voices, crawling under cages, and in and out and over obstacles. They called suggestions to each other, and whispered plans, as if he could overhear them, and they laughed at Valentine's impudence.

Finally, they had him.

"Companies pay money for this," Brendan said. "It's called team building."

It occurred to her they had been a team. And it had felt good. Why was it every time she was with him something happened that made her feel the delicious if guilty pleasure of not being alone?

Now she focused on him and the bunny. She could tell a lot about a person from how he handled an animal.

For a moment Brendan looked as if he intended to hand Valentine to her.

But then his expression softened, and he held the bunny firmly in the palm of his hand, his fingers tapered over the rib cage. He pulled him in close to his chest, stroking Valentine's snubby little nose with one gentle fingertip.

There was something about watching a strong man with a fuzzy bunny that could melt a person's heart. Nora felt some terrible weakness unfurl in her at his tenderness with Valentine, in his decision to come into the light. She was annoyed with herself for feeling as if she had unintentionally given Brendan a test, and she was just as annoyed that he had passed.

"Okay, I think I remember where the little

monster lives." He put Valentine back in the cage, closed the door and turned to her.

"Deedee's not going to take him home. I figured it out. She can't bear the thought of being with Charlie when he dies. Though I guess we're all wondering if he's going to die at all. He keeps improving."

"It's temporary."

"You sound certain of that."

"I am. I wish Luke wouldn't have taken it on. He's setting himself up for heartbreak."

"And he's had enough," Brendan guessed softly. "And so have you."

The look in his eyes was the one she had seen that rainy night when she had come to in the horse pen, when she had reached up and touched his cheek in welcome.

A person could drown in a look like that, throw herself willingly into those deep pools of understanding.

Instead, she congratulated herself for trying to back off.

"When you work with animals that are unwell, you expect a certain amount of grief. I've developed strategies for not getting attached. I don't name any of the animals."

"You named Lafayette."

She could say he had come named, but he hadn't. "Who would get attached to *him?*" she said, a bit defensively.

"How about Valentine?"

"Okay, so the odd one slips by my guard. But now that I have this beautiful facility, I don't ever let animals in the house. To prevent attachment, and also, where would you draw the line?"

"But Luke has Charlie in the house. And Ranger."

She bit her lip. "I know I should be stricter."

"But you took it as a good sign that he cared about something," Brendan guessed, and then reached forward and brushed her hair away from the bump on her head. "He cares about you. He told me he woke you up every hour on the hour."

"He did."

"And how are you feeling?"

"Exhausted."

"Funny, you didn't look exhausted when I came in."

She blushed, remembering that he had caught her dancing.

"In fact," he said, cocking his head, listening to the music blaring, "don't we have some unfinished business? Didn't you ask me to dance?"

Her mouth fell open. Of course she had not asked him to dance! He knew she had been talking to the bunny! What was he doing?

What was *she* doing? Because she found herself playing along, again. Boldly, almost daring him, she held out her hand.

Come, then, into the light.

And felt as if the bottom was falling out of her world when he took it. Because it was only then that she recognized what darkness she had been in.

Grieving her sister. And Vance's abandonment when she'd needed him most. Weighed down by extra responsibility. Wanting desperately to be everything Luke needed, and knowing in her heart she had been falling short.

She took Brendan's hand and smiled at him, and it felt as if for the first time in a long, long time that smile was coming straight from her heart.

What was he doing? Brendan asked himself.

Ever since that first smile had tickled her lips, a desire had been growing in him, and it felt as if his fate was sealed when she'd giggled today. When she'd laughed, chasing that bunny through the barn.

Brendan was not sure he could ever find his way to the light, or if the light could ever penetrate the darkness around him. He was not even certain he wanted it to, because it could mean the loss of the grip he had on the pool of pain inside of him.

Still, watching the cat change, watching Charlie playing, seemed nothing short of a miracle. What had he started to believe?

However nebulous he was about what he

wanted for himself, Brendan was aware of what he wanted for Nora. He wanted to make that light go on in her. He wanted something in her life to be fun and carefree.

It hit him like a ton of bricks what she needed, and why he felt so compelled by her need.

She was in the same situation his mother had once been in, a single parent struggling to be both parents, struggling to do everything right.

His mother's struggles had shaped Brendan, made him driven, made him want things for his own family that he and his mother had not had, and could not have even dared to hope for.

Now, looking at Nora, he could see the strain in her face, the stress in the droop of her shoulders.

It looked as if it had been a long, long time since she had laughed, or had anything approaching fun in her life.

The weight of the whole world seemed to be on those slender shoulders

It was not his job to lift it, Brendan Grant told himself. He'd managed to not get tangled in the web of life for a long time. Yet the last few days…

But that begged the question about the kind of man he had become. Hadn't he said to the boy last night that a mistake could be turned into an opportunity? To become something better?

Brendan had made a terrible mistake that night two and a half years ago.

He'd let Becky drive alone on a bad night. He should have been with her. She had begged him to go. She'd been so excited.

A pressing project at work. No, no, I'll meet you there. I'll come up later tonight. You'll wake up to my handsome mug in the morning. I promise.

He hated these thoughts. He hated that he was questioning himself. That he could see light, and was being drawn toward it. He hated it that he was coming back to life.

There was no reason he had to be here anymore. Nora didn't need him.

Except that she did.

Life was asking more of him. And there was

that ironic twist again. It was asking him to show someone else how to lighten up, how to have fun. But in doing so, he was coming closer to finding his own light. What if this time it broke down the walls all around him and pierced his heart like a lightning bolt?

It would be so easy to walk away from a challenge like that! But if he let the legacy of his love for his wife be bitterness, somehow he had failed.

If he could ignore the need of these two people, in a situation so like the one his mother and he had once been in, it wouldn't matter how many beautiful houses he designed and built.

What if the child Becky had carried had already been born? What if he'd had to figure out how to make a life for both of them *and* deal with his grief?

That's the situation Nora was in. She was grieving her sister and trying to make a life for her nephew.

If he didn't do a single thing to lighten that burden when her need was so obvious to him,

Brendan was not sure he would ever get the bitterness of failure off his tongue.

"So," he said, making a decision, cocking his head to the music. "Do you know how to jive?"

Ridiculous to feel as if it was the bravest and most risky thing he had ever done.

"No!" she stated, then asked skeptically, "Do you?"

"Of course not. Well, maybe a little. From high school dance class."

"Interesting school you went to! Word games *and* dance class," Nora said.

"Let's teach each other," he said. And then he pulled her in close to him. She put her hands up, pushing away from him, keeping a small barrier between her and his chest. She was tense and unsure.

Well, she should be. Maybe she was asking the question he needed to ask.

So he lightened her burden. And made her smile. Then what? What happened next?

But this moment stole his questions about the future. Her huge green eyes locked on his face, her pulse beating harder than that rabbit's in the delicate hollow of her throat.

"Relax," he heard himself say softly. He was still holding her hand, and rested his other hand on the soft curve between her rib cage and her hip.

She did relax, looking at him with fearful expectation.

"Okay," he said, "just like dance class. One, two, three, one, two, three."

They shuffled along the aisle between the cages. She looked down at her feet, her tongue caught between her teeth.

"I'm surprised you asked me to dance," he said. "You aren't very good at it."

"I thought I was pretty good when it was Valentine I was dancing with!"

"Uh-huh."

"I was. Not so inhibited."

"There's no cause to be inhibited," he said.

"Yes, there is! I'm going to step on your toes—"

"I can handle it. Steel toes." The truth was

he'd had to force himself to go to work today. He had wanted to be here instead. He had missed it here as he had not missed getting to Village on the Lake every day.

She glared down at his feet. "They are not!"

"Specifically made for construction sites. They are."

"I'm going to look foolish."

"There's no one here to worry about."

"What about you?"

"I'd love to see this—" he pressed a finger into the little worry line in her forehead "—disappear. Just give yourself to it. Just for a minute."

She hesitated, then he felt the exact moment she surrendered shiver up the length of her entire body.

"Now," he said softly, "you should try moving your hips."

"You first!"

"Just us and the bunnies. And a few cats."

"And a parrot who swears."

"Ah, Lafayette, the finger eater. Hard to find

a home for him, I assume?" The distraction of talking about the parrot worked. Brendan was moving and she was going with him.

"Hard to find a home for him? Impossible. Except for young men of a certain age who would take him to use as a novelty item at their frat parties. I couldn't allow that."

"That sounds just a bit like, um, attachment."

"Well, it isn't. That horrible parrot is probably going to teach Luke new words."

"There are no words that are new to a fifteen-year-old boy."

While she contemplated that, Brendan decided to up the difficulty level.

"I'm going to pull away from you, but keep holding your hand. Up in the air like this. Walk beside me."

"This isn't a jive," she said. "I think it's a minuet."

"Nope. No hips in minuets."

"Did you learn that in dance class?"

She was becoming quite breathless. He pulled her back to him, put his hand on her waist, leaned his forehead to hers. "Get ready to spin under my arm."

She did.

"Now spin back. We're good," he declared.

"We're not. We're terrible."

"Ask Valentine if you don't believe me. Get ready for the dip."

"Dip? No! Brendan! We'll fall."

CHAPTER ELEVEN

"FALL? ON MY watch? I don't think so. Relax. Trust me."

Nora giggled. Then relaxed, and then trusted him.

And at that exact second of giving her trust completely, his arm went behind the small of her back and she was literally swept off her feet.

Just like that she found her back arched, totally supported by his strength. Just like that they were in balance. In harmony. He held her suspended there. She gazed into his eyes. And then he pulled her in hard to his chest.

She leaned against him, feeling the steady, solid beat of his heart. They were both breathing hard, and she started to laugh. She laughed until the tears flowed.

"OhmyGod," she said. "I haven't laughed like that for so long!"

He was watching her intently, a little satisfied smile playing on his lips.

As if he had planned this. Give the poor beleaguered aunt a break from the monotony of her life.

It had been a nice thing to do.

But while she'd been losing control, he'd been gaining it.

And that was enough of that.

"Brendan, that was so much fun. I hardly know how to thank you."

Except that she did. She knew only one way to bring him totally into this place of light with her.

And before she could stop herself or think of the consequences, letting the momentum of the dance carry her, she was on her tiptoes, taking his lips with hers. And that's when the bottom really fell out of her world.

Brendan Grant's lips were like silk warmed through with honey.

Nora considered herself something of an expert on energy, but nothing could have prepared her for this exchange.

His energy was pure and powerful.

It swept through her, until it felt as if every cell in her whole body was vibrating with welcome for what he was.

A life force. Compelling. All-encompassing.

And that was before his kiss deepened. Taking her. Capturing her. Promising her. Making her believe…

…in the breadth and depth and pure power of love.

She broke away and stood staring at him, her chest heaving, her mind whirling, her soul on fire.

She didn't want to believe! Belief had left her shattered. Her belief in such things had left her weak and vulnerable and blind.

And she was doing it again.

Love! How could the word *love* have entered the picture? She hadn't given it permission! She hadn't invited it into her life! If anything, she was actively avoiding such a complicated twist to her already overwhelming life.

Realistically, she knew next to nothing about this man.

Except that he had known sorrow.

And that he was good to his deceased wife's grandmother.

And had given her nephew a chance.

And could hold a bunny with tenderness.

And could turn an ordinary moment into a dance.

And had made her laugh.

And was afraid of crumbling along with the walls that came down.

The truth was that Nora felt she knew more about Brendan Grant in less than twenty-four hours than she had known about Dr. Vance Height in more than two years.

"I don't know wh-what got into me," she stammered, and could feel the heat moving up her cheeks. She had kissed a stranger. It didn't matter that she felt she *knew* him. That was crazy. That was the illusion!

"I need to go. I need to go check on Luke. And Charlie. And your grandmother. And—"

"Hey!" He stepped in close to her, touched her cheek, looked deep into her eyes. "Don't make it more than it was. A spontaneous moment between a healthy man and a beautiful woman."

She stared at him.

It was nothing to him. Well, of course! No matter what she read into it, they did not know each other. While she was falling in love, he was building his walls higher.

"I—I'm not beautiful," she stammered. Of all the things she could have said, why that?

"Yes," he said, his voice husky, his thumb moving down her cheek and scraping delicately over her lip. "Yes, you are."

Because she had *needed* to hear that. Had needed someone to see the woman in her.

And for a moment she thought he was going to kiss her again. And she knew, despite her attempt at resolve, she would not do a single thing—not one single thing—to stop him.

But then he stepped back from her, shoved his hands into his pockets.

"How about if I start on the chores? While I wait for Deedee?"

Pride and a need for self-protection made Nora want to refuse. But if she said no, he would know that something he had dismissed as nothing had shaken her right to her core.

And practicality took over. As he had pointed out, her volunteers were largely little old ladies. Here was someone who could do the heavy work. She couldn't turn it down.

"Do you think I could get you to move some hay bales?"

"Sure, just show me what you need done."

Trying to shake off that awareness of him—a need that he had unleashed within her and that she intended to fight with her whole heart—Nora led him through the small-animal section.

She was going to pretend nothing had happened.

But it was harder, as she watched him walk through her world with easy familiarity, pausing to scratch a cat's ear, to stick his finger through mesh to tickle a kitten. Even the hamsters seemed to recognize him, and scurried to the wire to say hello.

They stopped in front of the colorful parrot, which at once swore loudly at Nora, using a term so derogatory to females it made her flush. Then the parrot switched to French.

Brendan's lips twitched. His voice stern, he said, *"Lafayette, fermez la bouche."*

"Ooh," she teased, unable to resist, even though she knew the dangers of teasing, "you speak French. What did you say?"

"Romantic gibberish," he said, wagging a fiendish eyebrow at her. "It means shut your mouth."

And the tension that had been building between them since their lips met exploded into laughter once again.

"What do you do with animals like Lafayette?" he asked when the laughter stopped. "The ones that won't be adopted for whatever reason?"

"I'm pretty new at this. I've only had the shelter open for six months. Demand for adoptable pets has outstripped animals coming in. I even found a home for a white rat! So far, that's a decision I haven't had to make."

"Maybe you should have a plan," he suggested.

She decided it would make her feel way too vulnerable to let him know how she dreaded the day she would have to make that decision, let alone plan for it.

They continued through the barn, and the dogs went crazy when they saw Brendan. With easy confidence, he moved into each pen and opened the door out to the run.

There were three dogs in residence, a black Lab with only three legs, which had been found out wandering. The cocker spaniel, Millie, had been brought in because her owner couldn't afford the diabetes medication. The puppy was of an unknown breed. A week ago he'd been a matted and flea-infested mess, wary of people. Now he gamboled after Brendan.

"I don't suppose you want to take one home?" Nora asked ruefully. "The dog with three legs?"

"You had me pegged right as a guy who wouldn't even have a plant."

It was a warning to her, whether he knew it or not.

Not a man to pin any kind of romantic dream on.

But she already knew that. She was so done with romantic dreams. Though there was something about being dipped over a man's arm that could breathe them back to life in anyone, even a more hardened soul than her.

And there was something about seeing him with animals that told the truth about who and what he was, even if he didn't know that himself.

"You'll have no trouble finding a home for this little guy," he said of the enthusiastic puppy. "I'm not so sure about Long John Silver over there. Really, you should have a plan."

"I don't want a plan!" she said. "What? After six months get rid of him? How could I walk by that cage every day if time was counting down?"

"That sounds a bit like attachment to me."

"Well, it isn't!"

It felt so much more powerful to be annoyed with him than it had felt being in his arms.

Finally, they arrived at a large stack of hay, and without being told, Brendan got a wheelbarrow and began to pull bales down. Nora went back to cleaning cages, putting in food and changing water.

Her annoyance, unfortunately, could not be sustained in light of how hard he was working for her. The awareness was roaring in her ears, sizzling through her veins. She could not help sneaking peeks at him. There was a certain poetry to a male body hard at work, and she was sworn off romance, not dead! Still, these kind of temptations—dancing, laughing, watching him pull eighty-pound bales down and shift them effortlessly to the wheelbarrow—were going to chip away at her resolve.

Thankfully, her cell phone buzzed, and when

she took the call there was a rescue she needed to go to. That was going to do double duty by rescuing her from the tingles on her skin and on her lips.

"Gotta go," she said, her tone deliberately breezy. "Iguana found on the loose in Hansen Lakeside Park." She ordered herself to thank him, and then to tell him not to come back. Diplomatically, of course. *Nothing here that Luke and I can't handle, especially now that school is out for the summer.*

But, weakling that she was, she found herself looking at Brendan's lips. She decided she needed to think about it before doing something rash and irrevocable.

Which probably described her decision to kiss Brendan Grant! Rash and irrevocable. Everything she did around him, from here on out, had to be measured and thought out carefully.

Everything she did around him now? From here on out? Hmm, not exactly the thoughts of a woman who was going to look at a man and tell him never to come back!

* * *

Three days later, Nora was scowling at her computer screen. Iguanas *did* eat dark, leafy greens. Except not the one she had. He was probably ill, and his owner had not been able to afford the vet bills. She made a note to pack up the iguana to take to her appointment with Dr. Bentley this afternoon. The vet was good enough to donate a few minutes to the animal shelter one day every week, and could also be counted on for emergencies.

She was aware that even as she did these routine tasks, her mind was not on them.

It was on Brendan Grant. He had brought his grandmother out every day for a few minutes, quite early in the morning, before he had to be at the office.

Nora couldn't very well tell him to stay away when Deedee wanted to see Charlie, refused to take him home, and couldn't drive herself.

Without being asked, without checking in, Brendan headed for the barn, and every morning after he left, Nora went out to see all the bales moved, the horse pen cleaned, the large bags of dog food organized, the aisle swept.

He didn't come to the house.

And she didn't go out. In fact, knowing now what time he came, she would sometimes scurry for cover just as he was pulling into the drive-way.

Though it felt as if she was fighting her inner demons. That spontaneous dance haunted her. As did the laughter. And his lips on hers. He was out there right now. She could just go down…

She heard the front door open, flicked her curtain back. She saw Deedee making her slow way back to the car, Luke holding her arm and helping her in. Brendan was nowhere in sight, but if she waited just a minute, Nora knew that he would be.

Then Luke came back in the house, and she heard him taking the stairs two at a time. She quickly flicked the curtain down and stared at her computer screen.

He stopped off in his room, and when he came up behind her a minute later, Charlie was drooping over Luke's crossed arms as if doing an impression of a leopard in a tree.

"Do the animals ever talk to you?" her nephew asked in a troubled voice, scratching Charlie's ears. "I mean, not in words, but you get, like, a feeling from them and know exactly what they're thinking?"

"Give me an example."

He took a deep breath. "Charlie is ready to go. He's tired. And he hurts. And he's a cat. Cats are clean. He doesn't want to be losing control of himself, if you know what I mean. You know why he's staying?"

She shook her head.

"Because he loves her. Deedee. And she's not ready to let him go."

In the past few days it was becoming apparent to Nora that Luke shared her gift, only his was a more intense version. Were animals really talking to him? Or was it just one more example of how her crazy decisions were affecting him?

Karen would not have approved of Luke being certain he knew what animals were thinking!

She had certainly never approved of Nora's abilities.

"Remember Mr. Grant said I had to make a mend?"

Nora nodded, not correcting him that it was "amends."

"That's how I'm going to do it. By getting her ready."

"How are you going to do that?"

"I don't know. But she thinks it's by mowing her lawn. I'm going to bring Ranger with me."

Nora gazed at her nephew, and he had a look of resolve on his face. Not like a boy, but a man.

For the first time in a long, long time, Nora didn't feel worried, even though to someone looking in it might seem as if she should.

Luke was communicating with animals! Or thought he was. That probably needed a psychiatrist, not what she was feeling.

He was taking on the gargantuan task of getting Deedee ready to lose her pet. It was a failure getting ready to happen.

Protect him.

But this was probably why her sister had wanted her and Vance as Luke's guardians. Because Nora felt proud of him for taking on the impossible. And as if there was a slim hope, after all, that her nephew was going to leave the world better than he found it.

Somehow the changes in Luke and her own feeling of optimism seemed linked, not to the wonderful summer weather they were suddenly enjoying, but to this man who was in her life while not being in it.

It was all beginning to feel like the scariest thing that had ever happened to her. In that nice scary way like anticipating someone jumping out from behind a bush at you on Halloween, or riding the biggest roller coaster at the amusement park.

Luke went to the window. "Brendan's coming up from the barn now. I'll catch a ride with him into town and mow Deedee's grass."

Nora wanted to scream no, the very same way she wanted to scream no as the roller coaster was inching up that final climb. But just like then, it felt as if it was already too late. She could see all their lives getting more and more tangled together.

Besides, when she looked at the simple bravery revealed in her nephew's face, Nora knew she had to be as brave as he was.

She joined him at the window and saw Brendan striding across her yard.

"He must change for work later," she said out loud, admiring the way faded jeans clung to his legs, to the leanness of his hips. A plaid shirt was tucked into his belt, but open at the throat. Her eyes skittered to the firm line of Brendan's lips.

She had to be brave. Whether she wanted to be or not.

"It's Saturday," Luke chided her.

"Oh. Now that you're on summer holidays, I forget sometimes."

"That's my flaky aunt. Who doesn't know what day it is?" But he said it with gruff affection, then added, "Gotta go. I'll call you later."

Luke put his hand on her shoulder, dropped

a casual kiss on her cheek. He squinted at the computer screen.

"It's not because we're giving him the wrong diet. Iggy ate something," he said.

"Iggy? Luke, we try not to name the animals."

"It's not really a name, just short for iguana. Dr. Bentley's going to have to x-ray him. How could an iguana swallow a house?"

And on that note, her nephew was gone, Ranger peeking out his hoodie pocket. He went back outside, and moments later, she heard him calling, "Brendan? I'll come with you. I'm going to mow Deedee's lawn. That's if Deedee can look after my kitten."

Nora twitched back the curtain just in time to see Luke hand Ranger to Deedee.

The old woman stared at the kitten. For a moment, she looked mad, as if she might give it back. But then her face softened, and she tucked Ranger into her breast and got into the car.

Brendan looked up at her, as if he'd known she was watching all along. He gave her a small

smile and a thumbs-up. As if they were raising this boy together. She let the curtain fall
back into place.

CHAPTER TWELVE

MIDAFTERNOON, NORA WAS thinking of Luke's words while she stood in Dr. Bentley's office looking at the X-ray of Iggy's digestive tract, and not his words about mowing the lawn, either. About how an iguana could swallow a house. The X-ray clearly showed a little toy house lodged in the reptile's digestive system.

"An iguana will eat anything," Dr. Bentley said.

The vet donated many of his services to the animal shelter, but was not volunteering an operation on an iguana, and she couldn't ask. Now what? They had a reserve fund, but to use it for an expensive procedure for an animal she had no hope of finding a home for?

She remembered being thankful, just days ago, that she had never had to face this situation.

Maybe you should have a plan. She hated it that Brendan Grant had been right. He had that look of a man who was always right. Who was logical and thought things through and never did anything impulsive or irrevocable.

We would be a well-balanced team, she thought, before she could stop herself.

"I need a minute to think," she said.

"Take your time."

She wrestled Iggy back into his cage and lugged him out to the waiting room. She had three choices. She could bring him home to die. She could have the vet speed up the process, which would be more humane. Or she could find the money for the procedure.

Her cell phone rang and she looked at the number coming in.

"Hey, Luke," she said, trying to strip the conflict she was feeling from her voice.

"It's not Luke. I borrowed his phone."

"Why?" It was him, the one who was always right. Maybe she'd call him that. Mr. Right. Then again, maybe not. She did not want to be thinking of Brendan Grant as Mr. Right in any context.

There was no Mr. Right! It was a fairy tale to keep females from empowering themselves! Ditto for thinking she was falling in love with him. Just another fairy tale.

"Because we're standing out in Deedee's yard and he handed it to me." A pause, and his voice lowered. "And because I wasn't sure if you would answer if you saw it was me."

"What would make you say that?" she said cautiously.

"I thought you were avoiding me."

Was she that obvious? It was embarrassing, really.

"Why would I be avoiding you?" she asked.

Silence. She thought of the boldness of taking his lips with her own, and shivered. She thought of the word *love* coming unbidden to her after she had kissed him.

He moved on without answering the question. They both knew exactly why she was avoiding him.

"I told Luke I'd take him for a milkshake. He did Deedee's lawn and then started on her shrub beds. They're pretty overgrown. He's worked really hard. I can't believe you've lived here six months and not been to the Moo Factory. His exact words were *'we never do anything fun.'*"

"We do fun things," she protested.

"Oh, yeah? Like what?"

We played a few hands of poker, once.

She knew it said something simply awful about her life with her nephew that, aside from that, nothing came to mind.

"We rented *Star Wars* last week."

"Really? That sounds like fun redefined."

"Are you being sarcastic?"

"It comes naturally to me, like breathing."

"We play Scrabble," she said triumphantly. "When I can get him away from the computer." Too late, she remembered they had invited Brendan to play Scrabble. He'd been unimpressed.

"Fun intensified."

She remembered his face that evening Luke

had suggested Scrabble. But she was on a mission now to prove they had fun.

"And Luke showed me how to play virtual bowling!"

"Wow!"

It let her know how wise her avoidance strategy was. He was sarcastic. It was hard to hold that fault in the forefront, though, in light of his good deed. He was taking her nephew for ice cream.

"I bet you threw the bowling ball backward."

"How could you know that?"

"Psychic. That should help me fit right in on the farm."

"Oh!"

"I warned you. Sarcastic."

"How did you really know? About the bowling ball?"

"I've played that game."

"Oh, so *you* threw the ball backward?"

"No." Suddenly he seemed impatient with the conversation. "Anyway, I thought I should ask your permission before I took Luke for ice cream."

It was so respectful it could make a woman forgive sarcasm. Or at least one who did not have her guard way up.

"That wasn't necessary. Of course you can take him." Ridiculous to somehow feel deflated that she wasn't being invited.

Then Brendan said, "Luke would like you to come with us."

Not *him*. Luke.

She looked at the sick iguana. And suddenly was overcome by weakness, not wanting to have to make this decision herself.

"I'm at the vet's office with Iggy, an iguana who has eaten something."

"Iggy," Brendan repeated slowly. "I thought you told me you didn't name them?"

"Who would get attached to an iguana?" she said, but the truth was maybe she already was. She didn't want to bring him home to die. Or put him to sleep.

She told Brendan what was going on. It was

his chance to say *I told you so,* but he didn't, and she felt it was another test he'd passed.

Another one that she hadn't meant to give him.

"You have a contingency fund?" he asked.

"Yes, but Brendan, that money would be so much better used educating people not to buy iguanas as pets. And the contingency fund isn't huge. What if I spend it on him, and then have an emergency next week?"

"On something with a little more of a cute factor than an iguana?"

She didn't mean to, but she started to cry. And she wasn't sure if it was because of the damned iguana that she'd been foolish enough to accept a name for, or because Brendan had gone virtual bowling with someone else who had thrown the ball the wrong way.

Or because it wasn't his idea to ask her out for ice cream.

It was Becky he'd played that silly game with. At a Christmas function? Everyone having hysterics at her lack of coordination.

He realized, holding the phone, that this was the first time he'd had a memory of Becky that made him *feel* anything. It was as if, after she died, he had started focusing on his failure to protect her, and that had erased all the good things from his mind.

But somewhere, had he also thought that thinking of the good would be *that* thing? That thing that would break him wide-open?

His contemplation of his treacherous inner landscape was cut blessedly short when Brendan heard a soft snuffling noise on the other end of the phone line. He tried to dismiss it as static, but the hair on the back of his neck prickled.

Maybe he *was* psychic. "Are you crying?"

The truth was his inner landscape seemed less treacherous than that.

The truth was he knew Nora Anderson had been avoiding him. And the truth was, he knew it had been a good thing. For them to avoid each other. Look at how quickly his intention to be a Good Samaritan by making her laugh had become complicated. By her hips under his hands. And then by her lips. On his.

"N-n-no."

But she was. Crying. Was it over an iguana? He was pretty sure she had said she was used to dealing with tragedy with animals. She had strategies for not getting attached.

Not that she seemed to stick to any of them!

An awful possibility occurred to him. Maybe it was because he had just thought of his wife that he was suddenly aware how quickly things could go sideways.

"Have you been having outbursts since you hit your head?" he asked.

"I am not having an outburst!" Now Nora was insulted.

Brendan was astounded that he felt guilty. When he'd been dancing her down the aisle of the animal shelter, he really should have been asking her concussion-related questions. And instead of doing the easy thing, and avoiding her and all the complications that her lips had caused in his uncomplicated life over the last few days, he should have been evaluating her medical condition.

"Have you been to see a doctor?" he asked.

"I don't need a doctor!"

"Look, outbursts can be a sign of concussion—"

"I am not having an outburst!" Each word was enunciated with extreme control, and then the phone went dead in his hands. Nora Anderson had hung up on him!

It seemed to Brendan that hanging up on someone could be evidence of an outburst.

Luke, flushed from heat, his hair flattened by sweat, came out of the flower bed, a tangle of bramble in his gloved hand. "Is Aunt Nora coming with us? For ice cream."

"I'm not sure what your aunt is doing." Except he was sure she was crying over an iguana. "Has she, er, been having outbursts?"

"What does that mean?"

"Crying. Snapping."

"Oh. You mean PMS."

Brendan wasn't sure if he should reprimand

Luke or not, but a look of such deep masculine sympathy passed between them that he just couldn't.

Luke seemed to contemplate the fact his aunt might be a little off today. "Maybe just bring me back a milkshake," he muttered, and disappeared into the garden again.

Then he peeked back out. "Can you get something for Deedee, too? And just a little dish of vanilla for Ranger. I'll pay for it." He glanced toward the house. "She's trying not to. But she likes him. Ranger."

There seemed to be a bit of that going around. People trying not to like each other, and liking each other anyway.

Luke was a prime example. It was damn hard not to like this kid.

And that went ditto for his aggravating aunt.

Knowing she wasn't going to appreciate it one little bit, Brendan made his way to the vet's office.

Nora was sitting in the waiting room, doing her best to look like a woman who would not cry over an iguana. The iguana was in a cage at her feet. It had a ribbon around its neck. Who tied a ribbon around the neck of an iguana they planned not to get attached to?

When she saw him, she folded her hands over her chest.

"I. Can. Handle. It. Myself."

"Uh-huh." It was the first time he'd seen her in a dress. Or in clothes that fit, for that matter. It was a denim jumper. She had amazing legs. It was kind of like Ranger, hard not to like something so adorable.

He ignored her glare and took the seat next to her. "Have you decided what to do then?"

He slid her a look. She gnawed her lip. He knew darn well that meant she hadn't. He remembered how her lip tasted.

What was he doing here?

Trying to do the right thing, he reminded himself sternly. Brendan took one more quick look at her, and then got up and sauntered past the receptionist and into the back to talk to Herb Bentley.

"Okay," Brendan said, coming back into the waiting room. Nora was fishing through her handbag, looking for tissues. "Let's go for milk-shakes."

While she was sipping her shake, he could grill her about concussion symptoms. He would look up a complete list of them on his iPad while waiting in line. There was always a line at the Moo Factory on Saturday.

She looked stubborn. "In case you've forgot-ten, I have to make a decision about the iguana."

"I've already made it," he said. He picked up the cage and put it on the receptionist's desk.

Nora bristled, balled up a tissue in her fist. "You made the decision? But you can't!"

It wasn't exactly an outburst, but it certainly seemed as if she might be on the edge of one.

Patiently, Brendan told her, "I told Doc I'd pay for the operation. Let's go have ice cream."

"I didn't tell you about Iggy because I needed you to fix it!" she said.

"Whatever."

"No! It's not whatever! I told you because I

needed a little tiny bit of feedback. I needed to not feel so alone. I trusted you. I didn't tell you because I needed the decision made for me."

She looked as if she wanted to stick her fist in her mouth after she admitted that. About not wanting to make the decision by herself. She had let it slip how alone she felt in the world.

He looked at her lips.

Well, that shouldn't last long. Her being alone. At the moment, she was the best kept secret in Hansen. When word got out, every unattached guy for a hundred miles would be beating a path to her doorstep. Brendan didn't even want to question the hollow feeling that realization caused in the pit of his stomach.

But only, he told himself, because he knew she'd made a bad choice once. Only because he knew it would destroy that kid up there slaving away in his grandmother's garden if Nora did it again.

Why was he worried about her? She claimed not to like attachments. On the other hand, she was already attached to the iguana, and God knew there were lots of lizards around.

"My paying for the procedure is no big deal," he explained patiently. "You could be having cognitive difficulties, postconcussion, that were making it hard for you to make a decision."

"I don't like iguanas. But that doesn't mean I want to have the decision whether he lives or dies in my hands."

"Well, now it's not. There. Solved."

"Oh!"

"Irritability," he said sagely. He knew it would be wiser to keep that observation to himself, but he was surprised to find a part of him was actually enjoying this little interchange.

"I am not having cognitive difficulties! And I'm not irritable."

He raised an eyebrow.

"It's justified irritability, not knocked-over-the-head irritability!"

"It just seems a teensy bit out of proportion. I mean, I thought you'd be—" he considered saying grateful, and then said "—happy. I just don't see that it's a big deal."

"You paying is a big deal. I'll pay you back," she said stubbornly.

"Consider it a donation."

"No."

"You really need a board of directors to answer to."

"And it's you making the decision that's a big deal."

"Wouldn't it be forgivable if I made the decision based on the presumption you might be having cognitive difficulties? Even if you weren't?"

He blinked at her. He happened to know he had eyelashes women found irresistible. He wasn't opposed to using them as a weapon when backed into a corner.

She stared at him. Blinked herself. Looked away.

"Talk about cognitive difficulties," she muttered. He was pleased that she suddenly lost her desire to argue with him. Still, she couldn't just give in! Let him have the last word!

"I will pay you back."

"Fine. I'll take it out in milkshakes. A lifetime supply. I like licorice."

"A lifetime supply? How much *is* the procedure going to cost?"

Seeing the worry creasing her brow, he cut the amount in half and was rewarded for his little lie when she looked relieved.

"There is no such thing as a licorice milkshake," she said.

"That just shows you've never been to the Moo Factory."

"Besides, if you think other people making decisions for you is no big deal, *I'll* pick the flavor of your lifetime supply."

It was all turning lighter. He could tell it was against her will. Maybe she *was* experiencing cognitive impairment!

"Have at it," he said drily. "I've never met a flavor of ice cream I didn't like."

"Apparently," she muttered. "Licorice? Yuck!"

He held open the clinic door for her and she went outside to the parking lot, eyed his vehicle suspiciously. "Where's Luke?"

"At the last minute, he said he didn't want to come. He asked us to bring something back for him so he could keep working. And he asked me to bring something back for Deedee, too. And Ranger. He said he'd pay for theirs."

"My nephew, Luke Caviletti, said he'd pay?"

"Yeah."

"You're sure? He's the kind of gangly kid with red hair."

But her attempt at humor was meant to cover something else and it failed. Her face crinkled up. She did a funny thing with her nose and squinched her eyes hard.

The facial contortions didn't help her gain control. He could tell she was making a valiant, valiant effort not to cry again. The tears squeezed out anyway.

He wanted to just shove his hands in his pockets and wait it out. But he was helpless against what he did next.

"Maybe…I…am…having…just…a…little… bit…of…cognitive…impairment." She was scrubbing at her eyes with that balled up tissue.

He went to her and pulled her against him, wrapped his arms around the small of her back and held on tight.

He could feel the wetness soaking into his shirt.

And the warmth oozing out of her body.

And her heart beating below his.

Now, for his own protection and for hers, would be a great time to confirm that emotional changeability was definitely a sign of concussion.

But somehow those words about the proven correlation between concussion and emotions got trapped in his throat and never made it to his mouth.

Somehow his one hand left the small of her back, went to her hair and smoothed it soothingly.

That feeling was back.

Of being alive.

Only standing there in the vet's office parking lot, with sunshine that felt warmer after the months of rain, with her body pressed into his, Brendan was aware he didn't feel resentful of waking up, of being alive. Not this time.

Not at all.

CHAPTER THIRTEEN

"OKAY," BRENDAN GRANT said, consulting his iPad. "Are you getting headaches?"

"You are spoiling the best milkshake I have ever had."

"Just answer the question, ma'am," he said, in a voice that reminded her of a policeman.

Nora leveled him a look that she hoped would get him to stop. He *was* wrecking a perfect moment. They were sitting at a picnic table across from the Moo Factory, in Hansen Lakeside Park. Iggy had been granted a stay of execution. Luke had actually offered to spend his own money buying another human being—and a kitten—ice cream.

The sun had brought everyone to the park. Children were screaming on nearby playground equipment, some boys were throwing a Frisbee, a young couple was pushing a baby carriage. Nora watched the small family and identified the emotion she was feeling as envy.

"They look like they would provide the perfect home for a three-legged dog," she said to Brendan when she saw that he had noticed her watching them.

"Now who is spoiling the moment? Can you stop worrying about your animals for one minute and focus on the question? Lack of focus! It's on this list of symptoms!"

"I seem to be getting a headache right now." Nora was trying so hard to steel herself against him, but honestly, when he turned on the charm? It was nearly hopeless. That thing he had done with his eyelashes? The big, innocent blink?

Criminal, really.

"I'm being serious!" he insisted, glancing at his iPad and then scowling back at her. As long as he didn't blink!

"So am I!"

"You have a headache?"

"Yes."

He scrutinized her, and looked as if he was going to scoop her up and rush her off to the hospital. Really, she didn't quite know what to do with all this chauvinistic caring.

What if she just surrendered to it? She'd had a bump on the head. She could be forgiven a weak moment.

"Could be brain freeze. From the milkshake," she told him.

"Ah." He looked genuinely relieved, but she wasn't letting him off the hook yet.

"Of course, it could be from being nagged by an exceedingly annoying man!"

His lips twitched a little, with amusement, not annoyance. He didn't look the least contrite. In fact, he consulted his tablet again. "I'm not being exceedingly annoying. I'm being mildly annoying. For your own good."

She rolled her eyes and took a long sip of her milkshake. Huckleberry Heaven really was heaven. But to be sitting across the table from a man like this on such a gorgeous summer day, and be asked about your cognitive function?

"Are you having any foggy feelings? Like you can't concentrate?"

Only when you blink at me.

"Would that be the same as lack of focus?"

He considered this thoughtfully.

"Can I taste your milkshake?" she asked him.

"I'm going to put yes for that one. What does tasting my milkshake have to do with feeling foggy?"

"I've never tasted a licorice milkshake before. I've decided to live dangerously, since a blood vessel in my head may be perilously weakened, getting ready to explode as we speak."

He glared at her.

She put a hand to her forehead, swayed. He furrowed his brow, baffled.

"My best impression of pre-aneurism," she told him.

She wasn't sure what it was, but he brought out something zany in her, a kind of lack of inhibition that she had not experienced often.

She liked it, especially when he shoved his

milkshake across the table to make her stop. Before he gave in and laughed.

She put his straw in her mouth. She was way too aware of the fact that her lips were where his had been. She thought maybe he liked it, too. He suddenly didn't seem nearly so interested in his silly questions. Instead, he watched her suck on his straw, and there was something so intense in his eyes it made her shiver.

"Whoo, that's cold," she said, to explain the shiver. She suspected he was not fooled. She pushed the shake back across the table at him. "Not to mention surprisingly good."

Deliberately, his eyes still locked on her, he took the straw. He was caressing the damn thing with his lips.

It was the closest she'd ever been to being kissed without actually being kissed. What he was doing with that straw was darn near X-rated. She shoved her milkshake across to him.

"Want to try mine?" she asked softly. She was encouraging him!

Apparently he did want to try hers. Intensity sizzled in the air between them as he grasped her shake, lifted it to his mouth, took the straw between his teeth and nipped before closing his lips over it.

"What else do you want to do?" he asked softly. "To live dangerously. Before the blood vessel in your head lets go."

The thing was, he was kidding. But the other thing was it was no joke. Life was not predictable. Her sister the health nut, dead in her early thirties. His wife in a car accident.

Suddenly, it seemed to Nora that she had not taken nearly enough chances. That she had not lived as fully as she should have.

If it was all going to be over, what had she missed?

It was easy to see the answer right now, with him sitting across from her, doing seductive things to her straw. The sun was gleaming in his dark hair; the faintest shadow of whiskers were appearing on the hard-honed planes of his cheeks.

She had missed the glory of being with a man like this.

And just letting go.

Enjoying wherever life took them, even if it was dangerous. Especially if it was dangerous!

"I want to rent one of those things down there." Nora pointed to a colorful booth and a dock. Parked beside the pier were flat-bottomed boats that had pedals in them.

She realized she wasn't kidding. She wanted to forget Iggy and a three-legged dog she could not find a home for. She wanted to forget an old lady whose cat, despite a reprieve, was going to die. She even wanted to forget poor Luke and the weight of her responsibility to him. She wanted to forget she had *Ask Rover* columns due, and bills to pay that relied on that column to pay them.

She just wanted to go out on the water and play.

"I think," she said slowly, "I want to live as if I'm dying."

"That's a song," he said.

She looked at him. She screwed up all her courage. "So, do you want to sing it with me?"

"Sure," he said, and it didn't even reduce her pleasure when he added, "So I can watch for more symptoms."

While he went down to the dock and arranged to rent the boat, Nora called Luke to tell him his milkshake was going to be late.

He said it was okay. He and Deedee had gotten tired of waiting and were eating pie, anyway.

"Don't ever eat pie cooked by someone really ancient," he warned Nora in an undertone. "I don't think she remembered to put sugar in it. It might be really old, too, like it's been in her fridge for three weeks."

"Don't eat it!" Nora declared.

"I can't hurt her feelings," Luke whispered, and then said good-bye and hung up.

She was still contemplating that when Brendan returned. Luke didn't want to hurt someone's feelings. It really was shaping up to be a perfect day.

"Okay, sailor," Brendan said, coming up to her and passing her a life jacket, "let's go."

Nora wondered if it was because they had been trapped inside so long because of the rain that they gave themselves so completely to an afternoon of playing on the water in the sunshine.

The boat, if it could be called that, was an awkward contraption. It was propelled forward, ever so slowly, by two people side by side, pedaling with all their might. Steering took some getting used to. There was no steering wheel. In order to turn the boat, one person stopped pedaling and the other kept going. The boat would start doing a painfully slow arc.

With much shouting and laughter she and Brendan headed out of the bay into the lake. They had not counted on the wind coming up and creating a tiny bit of chop. They had rented the boat for an hour, but by the time they got it back to the dock they had been wrestling with it, trying to get it back to shore against a headwind and a small swell for over two hours.

"Oh, boy," he said, "if that was your idea of living dangerously, I'd hate to see dull."

"It wasn't dull! It was fun!"

"Uh-huh."

"So, you pick something dangerous then, if you're so great."

"All right. I'll come for you tomorrow at ten."

"We're going to do something dangerous together? Tomorrow at ten?"

"Unless you're too chicken."

But she wasn't. She felt as brave as she ever had. That feeling lasted until the next morning, when precisely at ten, Brendan roared into her yard.

He was on a motorcycle.

It was dangerous all right, Brendan thought. They had taken the ferry across the lake and he was navigating the road that twisted along the north shore. It wasn't dangerous because the road had more dips and hollows and rises and falls than a roller coaster. It wasn't dangerous because of the tourists pulling trailers or boats

backed up the traffic, and the locals took incredible chances getting by them.

No, it was dangerous because Nora Anderson
was curled against his back, holding him hard
and tight, so close that he doubted a piece of
tissue paper could be inserted between them.
It was dangerous because instead of being the
least frightened, she was shouting with laughter and egging him on to new feats of daring.

They stopped for lunch at a pub midway down
the lake, and when she pulled her helmet off
and freed her flattened hair, her nose was sun-
burned and her cheeks were rosy from the wind
and she was shining with happiness.

She looked carefree and young, and he found
himself wishing that she would look like that
all the time.

Over steak sandwiches, on a deck that stretched
over the blue waters of the lake, they talked of
Iggy's recovery and laughed about Luke eating
Deedee's pie. Brendan told Nora about something funny that had happened at work, but was
aware of not saying a single thing about Village

on the Lake, which was supposed to be a pinnacle point in his career. She shared some of her ambitions for Nora's Ark with him.

It wasn't so much what they said as how he felt. Relaxed. At ease. As if he had known her forever, and she was the easiest person in the world to spend time with.

She sipped a beer; he stuck with water. Navigating the road, and his growing feeling for Nora, was going to take him having complete control of his senses! No impairment of any kind.

"You know what I did last night?" he asked.

"Cleaned licorice splotches off your shirt?"

"After that."

"Worked?"

He realized he was surprised that the answer to that was not yes. He always worked. But he hadn't last night.

"I looked up back columns of *Ask Rover* on the internet."

She blushed scarlet and took a swig of her beer. "Why would you do that?"

"Curious."

The blush deepened. "So, now you know. Nut job."

He frowned. "Are you kidding?"

"No. I never let anyone know I write that."

"But why?"

"All I ever wanted was to be normal. Not be laughed at. Not seen as eccentric or weird. I wanted to be popular and surrounded with friends. Instead, I had this thing, a strange ability to offer comfort to injured animals. My family used to tease me that I would have been burned at the stake if I'd lived in a different age.

"I can connect better with animals than people. It's kind of like mind reading, only without words. I pick up on the animal's energy. My family thought I was strange. The kids I grew up with thought I was a woo-woo. I learned to keep all that stuff that is outside the norm pretty secret."

"So, when you write *Ask Rover,* are you picking up that energy thing, even from a distance?"

She scanned his face, saw he wasn't mocking

her at all, but genuinely interested. "I'm not sure how much of it is picking up something from a distance, and how much of it is reading those letters really carefully."

"There are a lot of letters," he pointed out slowly, "from satisfied readers who are amazed by how applicable your advice is to their situation. How could you know that dog that had been shaking for a week had a broken tooth? How could you know that missing cat had gone in the appliance repairman's van?"

"They're just educated guesses…and a feeling. My weird little gift to the world. I hope you won't tell anyone it's me." She saw something in his face that looked stubborn. "It's for Luke's sake, too. So he can have a normal life here."

"What do you want for him?"

She sighed. "The things I couldn't achieve for myself. Popularity. A house full of friends. I don't want the fact that I do something different to make people laugh at him or judge him."

"You know, Nora, people make judgments. For instance, you know that dark period of history your family talked about, where they burned witches at the stake? They associated cats with witches, so they killed them, too.

"And when they killed the cats, the rat population exploded. And rats carried bubonic plague. Before that was over, twenty-five million people were dead."

"I'm not sure I get what you're saying."

"People make judgments. Lots of those judgments they make are just plain wrong. Somehow, we all have to find our own truth."

He hesitated. "I liked *Ask Rover,* but I *loved* the crossed out rough drafts that I read beside your bed that night. Does any of that stuff ever make it past the final cut?"

"No. Never."

"I wish it did."

She laughed, self-deprecating. "I don't think the world is ready for *Ask Nora.*"

"That's where I think you are wrong. The world could use a little more Nora at her brilliant, funny, insightful best. The world could use a little more of the real thing."

"If I cry are you going to ask if I'm h-having an outburst?" she stammered.

"No," he said. "I'm going to do this."

And he did the most dangerous thing of all. He kissed her. He kissed her long and hard and deep. He kissed who she really was, not the tiny piece of herself that she chose to show the world.

"I shouldn't have done that," he said, pulling away from her.

"But why?" she asked, her eyes round with wonder and wanting.

He shrugged. "We should go."

"No. I feel as if, when you read the columns beside my bed, you uncovered part of my heart, whether I wanted you to or not. That's not fair. Not unless you show me something of yours."

Brendan looked at Nora, and struggled with it. To show her who he really was. To crawl out from under the crushing weight of his guilt.

Her hand was suddenly on his. He could feel that energy of hers. Promising to lead him out of darkness toward the light, to roll the stone away from the entrance to the cave once and for all.

He still might have resisted.

If she had not proved one more time her intuition was uncanny. Nora said, "Tell me something about you. That's secret. Not just any secret. Your deepest secret."

He was torn completely, between not wanting to trust and for once letting his guard down. He had told her the world needed what was real about her. Could the same be said for him?

Nora knew things. She knew how to heal things. Look at Charlie. Just from being around her, under the same roof as her, the cat was pulling further away from dying every day.

So why had she asked this question? About secrets? The light in her eyes beckoned him in the direction he would not have chosen to go. The light in her eyes made him brave when he wanted to turn tail and run.

The long season of rain was over, and the sun had come out. Could his life be the same?

He took a deep breath. He told her something no one knew about him.

"I feel like a failure as an architect," he said.

"But you're very successful."

"I've never, ever, not even once stood in front of a house I've completed, and felt pride. I've always felt like I missed something. So there you have it, my secret."

She studied him for a moment. And then she said, "That's not really the secret. It's just the first layer of it."

"What?"

"I'd be willing to bet my newly repaired iguana that that sense of not being good enough has a root somewhere."

"It's not like I feel *I'm* not good enough!" he protested, but her gaze called him out.

He realized he hadn't even told Becky all of it, but been vague about his beginnings. Wasn't that part of how he had failed her?

"My mom was never with my dad," he said, and had to clear his throat to go on. "She got pregnant, he didn't care. She never said it, but

I suspect it was a case of unrequited love that culminated in a one-night stand. Who knows? Maybe she even used the pregnancy to try and trap him. But if she did, it backfired badly and left her young, uneducated and totally on her own. She was tired and bitter toward every man in the world except one, and that was me."

He shrugged, tried to laugh it off. "So there you have it, a genuine bastard."

There was something fierce in the way Nora was looking at him, as if she was seeing more, much more than he had intended for her to see.

"No," she said softly, "That's still just a layer of it. There's more. Tell me the rest."

This was her gift, then, unveiled. Her intuition calling to the broken place inside of him, coaxing it toward her light.

"We were poor," he heard himself saying. "There seems to be this little trend where its popular to say you were poor, poor meaning you didn't go out to restaurants to eat, or you didn't get forty gifts under the Christmas tree, or you didn't have the cool designer label clothes like everyone else.

"People who were really poor? They don't brag about it."

There. That was enough. He'd told her he felt dissatisfaction with his work. That he was illegitimate, and that he'd grown up poor. Those were his secrets.

But not all of them. And she knew. He could feel her energy pulling the words from him. Or maybe they had just wanted out for so long, they could not be stopped now that they had started.

Like the tears, if he ever let them fall.

"We were the desperate kind of poor. My mom worked as a maid at a motel, and in private houses, in the mornings, and a waitress in the evenings. Every penny counted. Sometimes we didn't have food. Sometimes we got evicted because we couldn't pay the rent.

"I grew up knowing it would be up to me to make my mother's every sacrifice worthwhile. She managed somehow—I have no idea how, and probably would have rather she put food on the table—to squirrel away a little money for me to go to university. I worked three different jobs. I got scholarships. She lived long enough to see me graduate.

"Once she died, I moved across the country to Hansen. There was a small architectural firm here. I told myself it was for a job opportunity, but I think it was to leave all that behind.

"And then I met Becky. To tell you the truth, I couldn't believe a girl like her would look at a guy like me. She had grown up extremely well-to-do, the daughter of one of Hansen's old rich families. She was the swimming pool in the backyard, vacation home at Vale, finishing school in Switzerland kind of rich.

"I slammed the door on who I used to be," he said. "I was ashamed of it. I didn't tell any-body what I'd come from, let alone this rich girl who was crazy in love with me. I thought if she knew it all, she'd never say yes when I asked her to marry me."

"But didn't she ask?"

"Of course she asked. I think, at first, she

thought it was part of my mystique that I didn't say much about my past."

He stopped himself. He was revealing way too much. No one cared about this stuff! But he looked at Nora, and he could see she cared. And he could see that the light in her eyes was not going to let him go, that he would not feel released until he told all of it.

"I felt I had to be worthy of Becky's faith in me. It wasn't enough to pay the bills every month. No. I had to succeed. I had to have all the trappings of success.

"When my boss decided to retire, we worked on my being able to buy the firm from him. And then, at the very same time, Becky's family home came up for sale. It was exactly the kind of house my mom had cleaned when I was a kid. She called them castles."

It was really time to stop. But it seemed as if that little boy who had promised his mother to buy her a castle was talking, and wasn't going to be quiet until he'd said it all!

"Sometimes if school was out for the day, or

I was home sick, I got to go with her to those fancy houses.

"For a kid who was living in a two-room shack on the wrong side of the tracks, that kind of house was a castle. A special room for dining? Four bathrooms? Hardwood floors and Turkish rugs and good art, and amazing chandeliers. The kids had bedrooms decorated in themes. In one house, the boy had a pirate room and the girl a princess room. I grew up on the phrase 'when my ship comes in.'"

It seemed to him he could stop right there. That he should stop right there. But it was as if a dam had broken inside him, as if something toxic was flowing out and with each word he spoke he felt cleaner and freer.

It was a free fall. He was free-falling into the light in her eyes, trusting that he could survive the landing. He took a deep breath. He was going to tell it all.

CHAPTER FOURTEEN

"BECKY, QUITE SINCERELY, didn't care if we bought that house. But I cared. I felt responsible for keeping her in the style she was accustomed to.

"I was stretched way too thin. I didn't want her to go to work. I felt that would make me a failure, mean I couldn't provide for her. I started working all the time, trying to make it all happen.

"She was becoming increasingly frustrated, trying to get through to me. She was beginning to see what she had mistaken for mystique was my inability to connect with her. She told me I wasn't fun anymore. That nothing was fun anymore."

And here it was, finally, the worst of it. The part where he'd killed a good woman who had done nothing wrong but love him.

"I didn't want to have a baby," he said, his voice hoarse from talking too damn much. "I thought it would just be one more stress. I didn't know she was beyond caring what I wanted. She was trying to save *us,* and I didn't even know we were in trouble.

"She'd booked us a ski weekend. Was I happy about it? No. Annoyed. Why was she spending money on frivolous things?

"But she wanted us to do something fun. She wanted us to be romantic. She had some big news to tell me. News worth celebrating. News worth spending money on.

"The day we were supposed to go, something came up at work. It seemed urgent at the time. Now I wonder if I made it urgent so that she would know I was still annoyed about spending money and taking the weekend off from work. I told her to drive up to the ski hill without me, that I'd meet her there later that night.

"She was upset with me when she left. It started snowing hard while she was on the road. She lost control of the car, skidded off the road and hit a tree. She was killed instantly. I found out her big news, the reason for our celebration, from the coroner. That she was pregnant. The baby died, too. She had stopped taking the pills. I know because I found them in our medicine cabinet after. When I was wondering if there was anything strong enough in there to end my misery, to end the endless question I asked myself.

"*Was* the fact that she was upset with me a contributing factor in the accident? Probably. And if work was everything before that, it was even more after. Aside from pills in the cabinet, it was the only way I could stop the guilt. The only way.

"You know, a week before she died, she said to me, 'If I die first, I'll come back and let you know I'm all right.'

"And I didn't hear the love in that. I just said, 'You won't be all right. You'll be dead.'

"She never has," he heard himself whisper. "She never has let me know she's all right. Because she isn't. And it's my fault that she isn't."

He waited to feel sorry that he had told Nora, sorry that he had exposed so much of himself to her, sorry that just as he now had a better idea of who she was from reading her column, she had a better idea of who he was.

He waited for her to say the wrong thing.

That he should absolve himself, or that Becky *was* all right, or that it wasn't his fault at all.

But she said nothing.

Nora didn't even look at him; she was looking out over the mirrorlike, serene waters of the lake. Her eyes were pools of deep calm.

He had to let her know who he really was. He had to. It was a compulsion he couldn't stop.

"I've never cried for her," he said. "Not the night they told me. Not at her funeral. Not once."

He thought that would make Nora yank her hand from his. But instead, her grip tightened. She left her hand where it was, and her touch had energy in it. Acceptance. Strength. Healing.

Suddenly Brendan felt an enormous sensation of freedom. He was still free-falling. It was the same as flying.

He had expected telling her would bring him to his knees, unleash that bottled-up torrent of grief.

Instead, it had given him wings.

From that moment of trust, an unexpected bond grew between them, and together they flew into the sun of summer.

They simply could not get enough of each other. Luke was part of the magic, somehow. Over Nora's sputtering protests, Brendan taught him how to ride the motorcycle in her driveway. And then he taught her. Just as with poker, Luke had potential, she had none.

The three of them sneaked away in the heat of the day to go to the beach and swim and play in refreshing, icy waters. They rented kayaks, which were more fun than the cumbersome pedal boats. They took the three-legged dog for long hikes in the cool of the forest.

With Iggy recovering under the kitchen table, and Charlie on Luke's lap, they played poker in the evening. Brendan even let himself be talked into Scrabble.

Increasingly, Brendan and Nora found ways to be by themselves. He took her to enchanted places, like the waterfall that cascaded out of the rocks on the Hidden Valley Trail. They ate picnics, and lay out on the grass, sometimes staying late enough to watch the stars pop out in inky skies.

Village on the Lake seemed the least important thing Brendan had ever done.

Important was reading over Nora's latest draft for her column. Important was taking Luke and Charlie to visit Deedee.

It was on one of those occasions that Brendan decided it was time to address the Charlie issue.

"Maybe it's time for Charlie to come back here to Deedee's. He's getting better." Brendan and Luke were doing dishes. Nora and Deedee were outside on her porch in the rocking chairs, Charlie on the elderly woman's lap.

"No," Luke said, and cast a troubled look

through the screen door. "No. He's not getting better. He's holding."

But given what Charlie had looked like just a short time ago, wasn't "holding" a miracle?

Brendan smiled to himself. He had gone from being the world's biggest cynic to believing in miracles.

That was a miracle in and of itself.

And wasn't that what love did? Create miracles? Turn the ordinary into the extraordinary?

Love.

Brendan contemplated that word, shocked by it.

But what else could make everything ordinary feel as though it was infused with light?

Even the hunger he felt for physical connection with Nora—holding her hand, brushing her hair away from her face, touching her lips— was a miracle of feeling alive, of feeling eager about life.

He took pleasure in showering her with little gifts: a gold necklace with two hearts entwined, a set of tiny silver hoop earrings. Girlie gifts that she was so uncomfortable accepting and then wore with such feminine pleasure.

He took her to public places, like Shakespeare on the Lake, in the natural amphitheatre at Lakeside Park. He had a barbecue at his house and introduced her to his friends and business associates. She still wouldn't let him tell anyone she was *Ask Rover,* though.

And it hit him right then, as she was standing at his kitchen sink, after all the guests had gone.

He went and put his arms around her, and breathed in deeply of her hair. She turned and caught him hard and they clung to each other.

And then she stretched up and he stretched down.

And their lips met right in the middle.

And he knew.

In the depth and passion and soul of that kiss, Brendan Grant knew the truth. He loved her. And he put her slightly away from him and he saw the truth shining in her. She loved him, too.

"I want to stay the night," she whispered.

But he knew that would never work for him. And it would never really work for her, either.

What he was feeling for Nora wasn't a one-night-stand kind of thing.

There would be people who said it was too soon, and that he couldn't possibly know, and that he was rushing things.

But it wasn't too soon. When he counted back the days, he realized he had known her for six weeks. Somehow they had become the best six weeks of his life. He did know, and in this life, where things could turn around so quickly, was there ever a moment to waste?

He had never in his whole life so badly wanted to do something right. He put her away from him. "You need to go home."

She looked wounded, and he touched her swollen bottom lip with his thumb, nearly caved in with yearning. Gave in to the desire to kiss her one more time.

This time when they pulled away they were both panting. His shirt was tugged out of his slacks where her hands had crept under it, splayed themselves across his flesh with an urgent wanting.

He broke away from her. "Go home."

Tomorrow he would go out to Nora's Ark with his motorcycle and pick her up. He would have the most gorgeous ring he could find in Hansen in his pocket. He would have champagne and strawberries, and he'd carry them to a viewpoint in the mountains where he could show her the whole world.

And then he'd ask her to marry him.

But for now? She had to go home before he did something that disrespected her and the enormous love he felt for her.

"Go home," he said gruffly.

He lay awake for a long time that night, thinking that soon his bed would not be empty. That soon his life would not be empty. He lay awake thinking of how he would propose. The exact words he would say.

He lay awake picturing the light that would come on in her when he went down on bended knee in front of her....

When he finally slept, he dreamed.

Becky had finally come to him. She was in a meadow filled with brown-eyed, wild sunflowers. She was in long skirt, and she was dancing, just like Nora had been dancing that day with the bunny. There was a blanket spread out in the grass, and a baby was sitting on it, his pudgy fist full of wildflowers.

And Becky was holding something, too, just like Nora had been holding Valentine.

Her face shining with joy, Becky whispered, "We're all right. Can't you see that we're all right? All of us."

And he moved closer to her, wanting to see her, wanting desperately to tell her how sorry he was for not knowing what he had when he had it. He moved toward her, needing to see the baby on the blanket and the baby she was holding.

But then he stopped short.

Because it wasn't a baby she was holding so tenderly to her bosom.

It was Charlie.

Brendan woke covered in sweat, to the sound of the ringing phone. He knew before he picked it up exactly what had happened. He actually considered not answering.

All this time he had been free-falling. Now he considered the possibility he was not going to survive the landing.

He picked up the phone. As he had known, it was Luke.

"Charlie's gone," he said.

Brendan almost said, "I know," but he didn't.

"You don't have to come," Luke said.

But he did. He had to go and be with them.

"I'll be there in a few minutes."

When he arrived, Luke was holding Charlie, with Nora sitting beside him, holding his hand.

She gave Brendan a beseeching look that said, *Take this pain away,* and he felt all the angry impotence of not being able to.

"I'll go out and dig a hole," he offered.

"No, I'm taking him to Deedee's." Luke said. "I made a box for him." He got up, carrying the lifeless cat, cuddling him against his narrow chest.

He brought back a box clumsily made of wood, the corners painstakingly sanded. It had a picture of Charlie lacquered onto the lid. Beneath the picture Luke had carved Charlie's name.

It was not a box that had been whipped up in the less than an hour since Charlie had died.

Nora lost control when she saw it.

But Luke didn't. He opened it up and laid the cat on the soft white towel inside. He put on the lid, and turned to Brendan, who felt as if his control was an elastic band being stretched thinner and thinner.

All this time, while he'd been having fun and romancing Nora and convincing himself love could fix everything and that the cat was going to get better, Luke had been getting ready for a different ending. A realistic one.

"We need to take him to Deedee's," Luke said. "I'll call her and let her know we're coming."

Considering how Deedee had had issues

around being there when the cat died, Brendan wasn't so sure that was a good idea.

"We'll bury him there," Luke stated, as if it was all decided. Brendan might have suggested they bury the cat here, but he was terrified if he opened his mouth all that would come out would be a wail of fury and impotence.

Silently, with Nora beside him crying helplessly, Luke in the back, quiet and pale, with the cat in the box on his lap, Brendan drove them to Deedee's.

She was waiting, dressed in black. Luke gave her the box, and she stared at it, ran her fingers over the carving of the cat's name, bent and kissed the picture. And then they all followed her out to the yard.

Brendan saw that while he'd been laughing, and packing picnics and buying trinkets, and watching stars come out, Luke had not just been bringing back a neglected flower bed. He'd been preparing a resting place.

The bed that had been such a mess was now fully weeded. Underneath a rosebush, Luke had dug a square hole. It had been there for a while; white rose petals had fallen inside.

Luke took the box from a quietly weeping Deedee and gently laid it in. A shovel was set unobtrusively against the fence, and he went and got it and began to fill the hole.

Deedee wailed.

It reminded Brendan of how she had sounded when they had buried Becky, that day he had stood there and not shed a tear.

Nora put her arm around those thin, caved-in shoulders of Becky's grandmother.

"Let's go in," she said. "I'll make you a cup of tea." They moved toward the house. Brendan stayed outside with Luke.

"I'll do it," Brendan offered, moving to take the shovel from him.

Luke's grip on it tightened. "No," he said, his voice fierce and strong and determined. "I have to finish it. I'm making a mend."

Brendan shoved his hands into his pockets and rocked back on his heels. He was so aware of his own stupidity. Over the last while, his guard had come down. He had let himself hope that everything could be all right.

In a world where it never was.

He listened to the steady thump of dirt hitting the top of that painstakingly crafted wooden box. He thought of Charlie inside, still and silent. Had he actually thought the cat was going to live?

Dead was dead.

He thought of how powerless he had been to stop anything.

Even falling in love, when that was what he knew he could not do. He knew he could not do it, because the light had broken through the cracks in his cave, undermined the strength of the walls.

Everything felt as if it was shattering around him.

Luke glanced up. "Are you okay?"

The youth was watching him way too closely, with that look so much like his aunt's. You could hide nothing from these two; they *saw* you, right to your soul.

Brendan pinched the bridge of his nose. He swallowed hard. He tried to breathe, and when none of that worked, he spun on his heel and walked away.

"Go home," Brendan had said to her. His face had been ablaze with love and with promise for a future.

But that had been before Charlie died.

She tried to think if he had said a single word at that solemn, sad little ceremony in Deedee's backyard.

Nora didn't think he had. And then he had left without saying goodbye.

There was no way she could have known that those last words to her had stopped short of the future. What he must have meant was go home, go away, it's over.

Those magical days ended as quickly as they had begun. Just like that, the phone stopped ringing, the motorcycle stopped appearing in the yard.

What had changed? Charlie had died. That

meant they needed him more, not less. At first, Nora felt furious with Brendan for letting them down.

This was when Luke needed to know he could count on someone else.

She needed to know that.

She had phoned and left Brendan a message. Had practically begged him to be there for her nephew. Had hoped he would hear her own unspoken need.

But he had not come.

Like a lovesick teenager, she had waited by her phone for him to call and offer some explanation, but no call came because there was no explanation.

Trying to protect Luke, she went through the motions. She even managed to rise above her own pain to think of Deedee.

She was bringing Deedee a casserole as Brendan was leaving. He saw her and searched for a way to escape. There was none.

He looked awful, as if he wasn't eating or sleeping. There were dark circles under his eyes and it made her want to go to him, wrap her arms around him and hold him.

But he was glaring at her, and then he crossed his arms over his chest, waiting, his face a mask. Holding him would be like trying to hold a porcupine.

She had to fight such weak impulses in herself, anyway. He had broken her heart. He had broken Luke's heart. And she wanted to comfort him?

He needed to be brought to task, and she was just the woman to do it!

She didn't bother with the niceties. She didn't say hello, or ask where he'd been or why he hadn't called.

She said to him, her voice low with fury at his betrayal of her and her nephew, "What are you hiding from?"

He smiled a tight, horrible, icy smile. "I don't know what you mean."

"You made a mistake," she said. "But not the one you think."

"Excuse me?"

"You think the mistake was letting Becky drive that night. But you had started to make the mistake long before that."

CHAPTER FIFTEEN

"WHAT ARE YOU talking about?" Brendan said.

She could hear the coolness in his voice, but he wasn't shutting her down or shutting her up. He was the one who, over the summer, had given her a voice, and now he would just have to live with the consequences of that.

"She wanted to love you. While you were busy trying to impress her with someone you weren't, she wanted to love you. That's why she got pregnant. She sensed you pulling further and further away. She wanted you back."

"You can't know that."

"I can."

"Stop it. You don't know anything about me."

"I know you're hiding. From pain. From life. From love."

For one full minute she held her breath. He

was hearing her. He was leaning toward her. He wanted it all: that place of refuge, the home, the love.

He wanted it all, and she could tell the exact moment he remembered the price. His face closed.

"That's rich," he said coldly. "This from the woman who never tells anyone who she really is?"

And then he turned and walked away.

The fury dissipated a bit that night as she contemplated that. She had taken a chance through these long days of summer. She had shown him who she really was. She had been zany and carefree, and she had let her intuition out.

Though maybe never quite so much as she had on Deedee's front steps this afternoon.

And she thought he had liked who she really was. Maybe even loved it.

But then, softly, it came to her. The point wasn't really what he liked or didn't like. The point was that *she* had liked it! She had loved it.

She had loved living in that place of freedom, without masks.

As long as she was hiding any part of who she really was, she recognized she would never have power.

She recognized something Brendan Grant might not have known.

You could protect yourself by being alone. But that required nothing of you. Life required something. And that was that you become who you really were, under any circumstance.

Life went on. Nora had a boy to raise. School was starting again soon. He needed school supplies and clothes. She needed to get on with the business of living.

She had even stopped writing *Ask Rover,* and now was very aware she needed to start again.

So on that first day of school, after Luke had gotten on the bus, Nora went through the piles of letters she'd received, and she didn't pick a single easy one. She didn't pick one that said, "Sambo will not stop pooping on the floor," or "Buffy attacks the mailman."

She picked one that said, "My dog is sick. Do I spend the money to make him well, or do I give up?" She picked one that said, "My kids want a dog so badly, but I'm a single mom and I feel overwhelmed already." She picked one that said, "I work long hours and am never home. Is this fair to my dog?"

She picked them, and with Iggy, the most lovable iguana ever born, snoozing on top of her feet, she answered them, from the place deep in her heart that had always whispered to her.

That place that other people didn't always understand, because it was so pure and uncorrupted.

It was a place of untainted instinct and uncontaminated intuition, and it was who she had always been and who she wasn't going to be afraid to be anymore.

And when she was done answering them, she changed her byline. It said *"Ask Rover, by Nora Anderson."*

When she was finished, she went out and visited with her volunteers, telling them there would be a meeting soon, and to please bring ideas about better organizing the jobs and having systems in place for dealing with difficult situations like Iggy.

When Luke came in, she was busy making cookies for him.

"How was your first day at school?"

"It was okay."

But she could tell it wasn't. "What happened?"

"Gerry wanted another fifty bucks."

"I'm calling his parents! This is outrageous. I should have called them—"

Luke put his hand on her shoulder. She realized she was looking up at him, and that he had grown a lot over the summer.

"I went to the police station at lunch hour. I told them the truth. I told them I stole the bike."

Her mouth fell open. He had grown a lot in every way.

"Did you tell them that boy is extorting money from you?" she sputtered.

"No," he said. "I just took away the reason he could extort money from me."

"I'm going to call his parents."

"No," he said, "you're not. I'm not giving it one more ounce of energy. It's finished."

"Are you going to be charged? For stealing the bicycle?" She could feel that old, desperate worry clawing at her. That she was doing it all wrong.

That she had let Brendan into their lives, trusted him, and now Luke was dealing with the loss of a male he had looked up to. And he was trying to navigate difficult situations on his own. Why had he gone to the police? He should have talked it over with her! What if he was charged?

"The sergeant I talked to said it was unlikely I would be charged."

Something was different about Luke since Charlie had died. Instead of tearing him down, it was as if the death of the cat had helped him come into his own, and in such a genuine way that not seeing Brendan did not seem to be bothering him.

Luke had used the word *energy* so easily a

moment ago, and suddenly, just like that, she could see his, and feel it.

Just like that, she knew who her nephew was, and who he would always be. She knew she had not done things wrong, after all.

Except maybe for one thing.

She realized he could handle an adult discussion. "I'm sorry about Brendan," she said. "I'm sorry that I let you become attached to him, and that he doesn't come around anymore."

When Luke looked at her, she realized he did so with eyes that were wise, the eyes of an old soul.

She knew in that second it was never going to be what she had hoped for him.

He was never going to be the popular kid, the one who laughed lots and was at the heart of all the fun.

It was never going to be like that.

It was going to be better.

He was introspective. Somber. Strong. Intuitive.

"Brendan not coming here is not about me," Luke said slowly. "It's not about you, either."

"What's it about?" she whispered.

"It's about hope. He hoped he didn't have to hurt anymore. When Charlie died, it reminded him he did. He was crying when he left Deedee's that day we buried Charlie."

Nora felt herself go very still. "Brendan was crying?"

"He didn't want me to see, but I did."

The words hit her like hammer blows. She'd been making it all about her. While she'd been breaking free, Brendan had been building up the walls of his prison.

And she had let him. She had accepted his strength. Accepted the fact that he wanted to be responsible for her and for the whole world. She had leaned on that, and come to depend on it.

She'd let him believe he was in charge of the whole world. She had relished that sense of being looked after!

And then Charlie had died, reminding him that protecting everyone and everything was a hopeless job. One he could not do. He withdrew, nursing the sense of failure and powerlessness that he'd had to face for the first time when his wife died.

"How'd you get to be so smart?" Nora asked Luke softly.

He snorted and was just a fifteen-year-old boy again, not a wise sage who had been born again and again and again.

"If you think I'm so smart," he said, snatching a still warm cookie from the sheet, "tell my math teacher."

Brendan stared down at the plan. It was after ten and he was still in the office. One of the fluorescent lights had started flickering a few hours ago, and now it felt as if his headache was flickering in unison with it.

He heard a door open somewhere in the building and ignored it. Janitorial staff.

He scowled at the plan, dissatisfied.

"You look happy."

He stiffened at the sound of her voice, straightened and glanced at the door. She was there. Her ginger hair caught the light and looked like a flame around her head. Her eyes were deep and soulful, and filled him with a sense of regret for the choice he had made.

To walk away. It was as if he had walked away from a pool of water beckoning a man who had crossed the desert.

But of course, he had walked away because he understood the nature of a mirage.

Even though he turned from her swiftly, masked that reaction of pleasure at seeing her, she did not go away.

She came and stood beside him, so close he could smell that cinnamon-and-citrus smell that was hers and hers alone.

He inhaled it as if it were that pool of water and he was that man dying of thirst.

"That's a pretty house," she said, looking down at the plan.

He ordered himself not to be drawn into discussion. To fold up his plan, fold his arms over his chest and drive her away.

But a man, any man, was only so strong.

And loneliness had made Brendan weak. He

would just drink in her scent and her presence for a while longer. A few minutes.

"The house is okay," he said.

"Really? What don't you like about it?"

It's not what he didn't like about it. It was what he didn't like about *him*. He used to focus only on the house, and the function of it. He had never wondered about the lives that would be lived inside.

"It's a pretty house, for a lovely young couple."

"And?" she prodded.

"They've never known a moment's agony over anything."

"And?"

"And I hope they never do."

"But?"

"But I doubt it, because life doesn't go that way."

"That's right, it doesn't," she said, ever so gently, just as if he hadn't let her down. As if he hadn't let Luke down.

"That little baby they loved so much, that they

were cooing over and bouncing up and down on their knee while they sat across from me in my office?"

"What about the baby?"

"It will probably take them through the fires of hell one day. It could get sick, or experiment with drugs, or get bullied at school."

"That's what love does," she said, as if she was agreeing with him. "It leaves you wide-open to all kinds of pain."

"And this pretty little house wouldn't help any of that. It won't help it and it won't stop it."

"No," she agreed, "it won't. Because you don't have that kind of power."

"We're not talking about me."

"Yes, Brendan, we are—the one who builds houses, the one who chose to build houses because he always longed for a home. The one who wanted so badly for that home to protect all who enter there."

"Why are you here?"

"I've come to take you home. Not to a house. I've come to take you home to my heart."

"See?" he said with a snort of pure derision, doing what needed to be done, trying to wound her, trying to drive her away. "They were all right about you. You are a pure flake."

"Yes," she said sweetly. "Yes, I am. But I'm your flake."

"You're not my flake. I don't need a flake."

"You do. Desperately."

"What could you possibly know about my need?"

"Everything."

He scowled.

"I'm intuitive, remember? A healer. I know what you need."

Don't even ask her, he ordered himself. "What do I need?" he asked, masking his desperation with a sneer.

"You took a chance," she said. "You loved. And you felt as if it made you weak instead of strong."

Accurate, but not spookily so. He kept his arms folded over his chest, his expression cynical.

"You need a place," she said softly, "where you can put away your armor."

His mouth fell open. He clamped it shut.

"You need a place where you don't always have to be the strong one. Where it's okay to fall when the parachute doesn't open."

Now it was getting spooky.

"Where someone is going to be there to catch you."

"It sounds like a good way to get squashed like a bug on a windshield," he said.

"That's exactly how I'd want to go."

"Like a bug on a windshield?" he said cynically.

"In the service of love," she said simply. "You'll need a strong woman, Brendan. A relationship not based in her need and you providing, but based in true equality.

"Based in the recognition that, on some days, you'll hold her up, and other days, made strong by your love when she needed it most, she will hold you up.

"I'm that woman."

She sounded absolutely certain.

"I love you," Nora said with quiet composure. "And I'm never stopping. Not if it hurts me. Not if you won't let me. I'm still going to love you. I'm going to be wide open, and if it brings pain, I'm ready to accept that as part of the price of living fully, not tucked away in a cave somewhere."

He knew he had never said a single word about a cave to her. Never.

"So," she finished, her courage shining from her eyes, enough courage for both of them, "you might as well come along for the ride."

"You're crazy."

"I know," she said. "Ask Rover."

He fought the impulse to smile, but he had to fight hard.

And then she did the one thing he could not fight. The one thing that stole what remained of his strength.

She moved in close to him. She slipped her hand behind his neck and pulled his face to hers. She searched his eyes and found what she wanted there, because she smiled.

He recognized it instantly, identical to that very first smile he had seen from her when he had turned over a pile of rags in a paddock on a rainy night. It was a smile that knew exactly who he was and welcomed him.

And then she kissed him.

And he, weakened, kissed her back.

Only, the strangest thing happened. As her lips laid claim on him, his surrender became not weakness, but strength.

It felt as if she had somehow captured every one of those tears he had cried after that damn cat had died. She had captured them, and now she poured them back into his emptiness.

The energy washed off of her, and into him. Brendan could feel the life flowing back into his body, like water over parched earth.

He could feel himself opening instead of closing.

He could feel himself becoming everything

he was ever meant to be, and then more. More than he had ever hoped he could be.

He lifted her slight body to him, and cradled her against his chest.

This was his home. This was what he had struggled to capture with his building designs his whole life, and this was why he had always had a sense of failure.

Because the most essential thing had been missing. Home was not a building. It was the spirit that filled it.

EPILOGUE

BRENDAN SAT BESIDE Nora in the crowded Hansen High School auditorium. They had endured the speeches, and with each one being duller and longer than the last, he wished Nora, Hansen's most celebrated citizen, had accepted the invitation to speak.

Once she had changed her column to *Ask Nora,* amazing things had begun to happen. The internet blog had been a sensation. A book of her columns and blogs had followed, and it had been on the bestseller list for eight straight months. And then she'd been approached to do a radio show.

So, as Hansen's most celebrated citizen, Nora had been asked to give the commencement address at the high school graduation.

But she had said no—it was Luke's day, not

hers. Which had been a relief to Brendan, be-cause what if the baby decided to come mid-speech, and they had to leave fast?

They had long since sold Brendan's house on "the Hill."

When the acreage next to Nora's became available, they had purchased it. They had worked on the plan for the new house together. It wasn't the biggest house he'd ever built, and it certainly wasn't the grandest.

And yet it was filled with the secret that made a house something beyond a collection of sticks and stones. It was filled to the rafters with laughter and companionship and healing. Somehow Lafayette had made it in there, and so had Iggy. And the dog with three legs, who came when they called "Long" or "John" or "Silver." There was a descendant of Valentine named Cupid, and Ranger, and a small pasture that contained two sheep, Bo and Peep, and a burro named Burrito.

Nora's property had been sold at cost to Nora's Ark, now registered as a charity, with a board of directors and an army of volunteers running it. Though she still crossed the fence when a sick animal arrived in the middle of the night, even if she had not been called. She always knew a new animal had arrived, always knew when her special gifts were needed.

And more often than not, Luke was right beside her.

As each name was read out, a graduate walked across the stage.

It occurred to Brendan you could tell a lot about these kids from the way they crossed that stage. You could tell if they were shy. Or outgoing. Or plain old trouble. You could tell by the way they walked if they were going to be ambitious or complacent, if they were going to take the world by storm or just ride a lazy current through it.

"Ohh," Nora sighed quietly beside him.

He turned and looked at her, ready if need be to disrupt the ceremony, to pick up his wife, just the way he had picked her up all those years ago, and race for the door.

But she gave him a reassuring smile and placed his hand on the swell of her stomach. The baby kicked at his palm, as if impatient to make its entrance into the world. One day he or she would be crossing this stage. What would the way he or she walked say about all of them who had helped raise this child?

Brendan had deliberately chosen aisle seats. Now he glanced back toward the door, making sure the way was clear, judging how long it would take him to reach it with Nora in his arms.

But Nora and Luke had both assured him today was not the day, and for a reason Brendan still could not decipher, they knew these things. But still, he needed to be prepared. They had their way, he had his.

"Luke Caviletti."

Brendan turned his attention fully to the stage.

He had offered Luke his name a year ago, but Luke had said no. He didn't need the name to feel he was a valued part of the family. He had wanted to carry his father's name into the future.

As he came across the stage, that was what Luke looked like, a beam of pure light heading for the future. Brendan hadn't expected to feel anything at this graduation except too warm and bored, so his sudden emotion took him by surprise. He didn't try to pinch his nose, or swallow, or breathe it away. He just let it come, grateful to feel, to be alive, to have this moment of glorious pride and emotion.

He had helped raise this young man, and through the tears that blurred his vision, he could see every single thing about him.

Out of the corner of his eye, he saw the tears of joy and pride sliding down Nora's face, also. Brendan moved his palm from her stomach, took her hand in his and squeezed ever so gently.

Luke had never become what Nora had dreamed of—the popular kid who filled up their house with his friends and noise and activity.

What he had become was so much better.

He had become himself: strong, quiet, calm, certain in the gift he had to give the world. Neither Nora nor Brendan had been surprised when this young man, once terrified of hospitals, told them he would use the money Deedee had left him to become a doctor.

Luke had that same incredible quality that Nora had, the one that made people call her a healer. Only in him, it was more intense, more defined, something tangible in the air around him.

When Brendan had first met Nora, she had just lost her sister. And her fiancé. And yet despite that, she had never hesitated to be of service. She had been there for her nephew. She had provided a place of refuge for the lost and wounded of God's creatures.

Luke had that same ability to rise above what had hurt him, and use his life experience in service. He would make an unbelievable doctor.

And Brendan was learning from both of them. Village on the Lake was completed. People had moved in. They loved it there. It had won a Most

Livable Community award. But now he understood exactly why all those early plans had always left him dissatisfied.

He had tried to use his work to shore up a wounded ego in service to nothing more than himself.

There was no satisfaction in that, no matter how many awards you won.

But today a different plan took center stage. He was designing a housing complex for single parents of limited income. It wasn't utilitarian or bare bones. It was beautiful.

Nora had been right. He had embraced the science of architecture with his mind, but his heart had always known it would lead him where he was meant to be. For what he really wanted was to create *home*.

Not just for him and Nora, for the baby and Luke.

No, for those afraid to dream. For those who had nothing to hope for. For those who had been abandoned, who had been crushed and were afraid.

The housing complex Mary Grant Court bore the name of his mother. Brendan loved it. He woke up every day filled with energy, excited to go to work, happy in a way he had not even known it was possible for a man to be happy.

Energy was really not the mystery he had once thought it was. You could see its power in a thunderstorm. It was energy harnessed when you turned on a light. Energy ran through each amazing thing on the planet Earth, all those invisible particles of matter moving so fast they gave the illusion of being solid.

But there was a place where energy transformed. And that place was the great mystery. It didn't remove pain; it married it. It didn't alter life experience; it merged with it. It fused with all things and became something larger than itself.

And that was when it became more than energy.

Then it became a force that could turn a pile of lumber and a load of concrete into that most blessed of places, a home.

Then it became the force that could heal the broken.

Then it became the force that could raise the dead.

Many people called it many things.

Brendan called it love.

And knew that he was the most blessed of men that he had been allowed to know it.

* * * * *

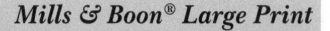

Mills & Boon® Large Print
November 2013

HIS MOST EXQUISITE CONQUEST
Emma Darcy

ONE NIGHT HEIR
Lucy Monroe

HIS BRAND OF PASSION
Kate Hewitt

THE RETURN OF HER PAST
Lindsay Armstrong

THE COUPLE WHO FOOLED THE WORLD
Maisey Yates

PROOF OF THEIR SIN
Dani Collins

IN PETRAKIS'S POWER
Maggie Cox

A COWBOY TO COME HOME TO
Donna Alward

HOW TO MELT A FROZEN HEART
Cara Colter

THE CATTLEMAN'S READY-MADE FAMILY
Michelle Douglas

WHAT THE PAPARAZZI DIDN'T SEE
Nicola Marsh

1013 Rom LP

Mills & Boon® Large Print
December 2013

THE BILLIONAIRE'S TROPHY
Lynne Graham

PRINCE OF SECRETS
Lucy Monroe

A ROYAL WITHOUT RULES
Caitlin Crews

A DEAL WITH DI CAPUA
Cathy Williams

IMPRISONED BY A VOW
Annie West

DUTY AT WHAT COST?
Michelle Conder

THE RINGS THAT BIND
Michelle Smart

A MARRIAGE MADE IN ITALY
Rebecca Winters

MIRACLE IN BELLAROO CREEK
Barbara Hannay

THE COURAGE TO SAY YES
Barbara Wallace

LAST-MINUTE BRIDESMAID
Nina Harrington

1113 Rom LP